KNEE HOLES

 A RICHARD JACKSON BOOK

Also by Jerome Brooks

Uncle Mike's Boy
The Testing of Charlie Hammelman
The Big Dipper Marathon
Make Me a Hero
Naked in Winter

Knee Holes

Jerome Brooks

ORCHARD BOOKS

NEW YORK

Orchard Books, 387 Park Avenue South
New York, NY 10016

Manufactured in the United States of America
Book design by Mina Greenstein
The text of this book is set in 12 pt. Sabon.
10   9   8   7   6   5   4   3   2   1

Library of Congress Cataloging-in-Publication Data
Brooks, Jerome. Knee holes : a novel / by Jerome Brooks.
p.   cm.   "A Richard Jackson book"—Half t.p.
Summary: Infatuated with the teacher who placed her
in an honors program, fifteen-year-old Hope becomes
spokesman for the gifted students when trouble appears
to be simmering between that teacher and another in
the program.
ISBN 0-531-05994-4   ISBN 0-531-08594-5 (lib. bdg.)
[1. Gifted persons—Fiction.   2. High schools—Fiction.
3. Schools—Fiction.   4. Teachers—Fiction.]   I. Title.
PZ7.B7953Kn   1992   [Fic]—dc20   91-25398

To ELLEN RUDIN for "Charlie"
    and
to DICK JACKSON for "Hope"

*"Whatever gains I ever made
were always due to love
and nothing else."*

SAUL BELLOW:
Henderson the Rain King

KNEE HOLES

1

SHOOT, I hate being late!

Dr. Rogers said, "Three will be just fine, Ms. Gallagher."

But here it is nearly three-thirty.

It being the Thursday before Christmas vacation, I suppose I could've tried harder to keep out of trouble and get the holidays off to a proper start.

Now, despite my wheezing up the stairs two at a time, there's no way I'm going to make up for the twenty minutes I wasted in detention because of cutting stupid gym again.

Brother!

'Course, I suppose I could have said to him, "Dear, revered, adored Dr. Everett Rogers, no need to hurry. I can wait until after the holidays to see what grade I got on my very first *long* English honors paper."

But with less willpower than a wooden weather vane, who am I kidding?

If I hadn't asked whether I could get that paper back before the holidays and if he hadn't said, "Certainly," Lord only knows what I would've done the next two weeks.

But it kills me anyway to keep *him* waiting.

What the man wrote last month on my Sylvia Plath paper will live in my memory forever: "You show an enviable sensitivity to the plight of other human beings—as attested by your attire."

I don't care if he *was* referring to my stone-washed jeans with the holes at the knees or not.

It's the nicest thing a teacher has *ever* written or said to a sophomore at Livingston Magnet High School.

Or *anywhere!*

My chest's heaving like a bellows when I reach Room 272, his office, in what's called the Levian Wing of the building. (Levian is the school's coined nickname.) The door's ajar, and there—my God!—he is, standing just beyond it, glorious, regal, statuesque. His back is to me.

"Ahem," I say. I hesitate to call him Doctor, though like a uniquely high percentage of other teachers at Livingston Magnet, he has a Ph.D. Unlike most of them who *require* you to, he insists it's a little pretentious for high school teachers to be addressed as Doctor when most of them would faint at the sight of blood.

Still and all, for weird reasons, his resistance makes me all the more determined. "Ahem, Dr. Rogers . . ."

At the sound of my voice and the *squick-squack* of my shoes, he turns. His shimmering teal blue eyes catch me.

And his voice—ah, his voice!—soars, in words like eagles, "Ms. Hope Gallagher, I'd almost given up on you."

His loud tie clashes horribly with his large-checked sports jacket.

But so what?

If anything, the teal blue eyes and long hair create an aura of dignity around him.

And *aura*, sadly, is something few of his colleagues these days share.

His hair swings from one jacket lapel to the other.

I quiver as usual.

I know!

I've been in his class four months, and I shouldn't quiver anymore. But just as I can't explain how a computer glitch put me in his honors English, *my first honors class ever*, so I can't explain the quiver.

Compared to my older sister, Heather, and my younger brother, Matthew, who seem to have been in honors classes most of their lives, I have accomplished *nothing* academically.

I stammer. "Er . . ." I'm getting ready to lie, to say I've been tied up with legitimate educational business.

But the twitch that twitched in me when I first saw and heard this man twitches still and stops me.

"I cut gym this A.M. Had to pay the consequences."

He destroys me with a smile.

"I know exactly what you mean. Nonsense like gym is hard to take on a regular basis."

He fumbles in his briefcase.

If my theme, "Language as Man's Last Hope," is less than he expected, life's not going to be worth living.

If it's as much as he expected, I may never return to normal.

If it's *more* than he expected, they may have to come and lock me up.

Me a winner? The person my psychologist father and sociologist mother have always perceived as an underachiever?

You've got to be kidding!

His fingers, like budding tulips, emerge from the depths of the briefcase, grasping my ten-page paper.

The month I spent hovering over it, grooming it, fondling it in the privacy of my room on the second floor of our Victorian house on Sandalwood Drive, returns to me in a vision. There, by the window overlooking the forest preserve, I sat entranced by the russet and golden fall leaves and felt how precious life was . . . is! . . . in . . . in . . . Dr. Rogers's class.

And now he has that life in his hands!

He bows low, his hair swooshing, and hands the paper to me, grade down. When he straightens up, he smiles and says, "Beautiful paper, young lady. Top-notch job of thinking."

Lord Almighty! Dear God!

"Oh," I say, fiddling with my split ends.

I can't look him in the eye.

How would I dare?

How'd I hold myself together?

I'd like to say, "Dr. Rogers, I don't know what I'd do without you."

But no. I can't!

Instead, I mutter this moronic "Thank you very much, Dr. Rogers."

I'm in spasms. I spin around to leave.

The tiny voice whispers to me, *Wish him a happy holiday, for God's sake!*

But Lord! He's a married man. With at least one child that I've heard of.

What would his wife think?

His voice reaches out to me over my shoulder and snares me with this: "Hold on there, won't you? I've got a question." I've stepped only two or three feet toward the door.

My heart fibrillates.

But I turn anyway.

Since I'm a good head shorter than he, I focus on

the blue and red rhombohedrons lying tip to tip on his tie. They are like stained-glass church windows shot through by golden sunlight on a summer day.

"There's this program I've designed," he starts.

My body tightens all over.

"A block program, team-taught by me and four others, plus a counselor, that's going to mix the sciences and the arts. We want to wind a single thread of unity through all the separate disciplines. What we'd like to find out is whether the quality of thought that leaders of the twenty-first century will require needs to be stressed a good deal more than the quantity. The steps involved in the thinking process itself are critical." He winks. "Are you interested?"

Am I interested?

Does the moon circle the earth?

Is Mars red?

Do hummingbirds hum?

But Lord!

How can an idiot like me compete with the geniuses in this school?

I'm in his class because of a computer glitch!

Clutching my "Language" paper, I say the first thing that comes to me.

"I'm flattered, Dr. Rogers, but I'm afraid I can't. I work after school."

Sure, it's blasphemy to lie to him!

And I wouldn't—normally.

But this isn't normal, dear God!

School's always bored me. My folks know that. Every past and present teacher—except him— knows it.

Science and the arts—let's say nothing about becoming leaders of the twenty-first century!—make me reel.

Dr. Rogers, though, won't let loose.

"If I remember correctly, Ms. Gallagher," he says, "you also turned me down before—when I handed out that list of paper topics. After I suggested that you pick the one on language, you tried copping out, too. Remember? We had, as I recall, a minor discussion about something called 'massive perseverance.' Did that discussion pay off or not?"

I didn't think he'd remember.

He stares at my jeans.

"This poor self-image you have, I do believe we can work at improving." He takes hold of his lapels and tugs them vigorously. "Like my jackets and ties, the knee holes in your jeans give you away as an exceptional misfit among robots, a latent bloomer, exactly the kind of student this program will help and will be helped by. All of us, working together, ought to be able to reinforce one another's self-esteem through emotional and intellectual challenges . . ."

The blood rushes hot and red to my cheeks. My hair—under the best of conditions leaving much to be desired—frizzes with each and every one of his words.

He's seen right through me. My having to work after school obviously has *nothing* to do with turning him down.

"... so that we'll see we *can* do those things we have the potential to do. Yes! And actually do them better, far better than we ever believed possible."

He homes in on me now, determined to shatter me into a million chunks.

"How about it? Are you interested in being part of this pilot honors program?"

Thank God he can't see the goose bumps tingling along my arms. My ten-page paper, soaking wet inside my clenched fist, doesn't matter anymore.

I swallow the knot in my throat and say, "When do I have to let you know?" as if I didn't know already what my new answer will be.

He breaks into another devastating grin.

"If it's true that the best defense is a good offense, then maybe it follows that the way to beat your impulsive self-deprecation is to be impulsively positive," he says. "In other words, young lady, I want your answer now ... before I pick the other nineteen students for the program."

Shoot, if that doesn't settle it!

He's picked *me* first!

"Then the answer's yes, Dr. Rogers." What I can't tell him is that if it turns out I disappoint him, I'll plain up and die!

It's four o'clock, and by the time I get to Wardman's Merchandise Center downtown, I'm half an hour late for work and may be reminded once more by Danny Stewart, the manager, that I have no sense of responsibility.

But so what?

Dr. Everett Rogers thinks I do!

2

THE NEXT COUPLE of hours at Wardman's pass like a dream.

While I'm checking people out at my register, I'm thinking about what it is I've gone ahead and gotten myself into. With each new customer, my feelings rise and fall like a roller coaster.

Faces and carts and packages and voices come at me through the checkout like bullets from a machine gun.

It's a nightmare!

My arms flail this way and that through the onslaught.

I've got to get home.

For once, I have *good* news to announce.

When I float through the front door and hang my jeans jacket up on the clothes tree, everyone's already seated for dinner.

"Hi," I say.

My father, too, stares at the holes in my jeans. We have been this route before, he and I.

Heather's jeans don't have holes. Why should mine?

"Hi," he says.

I love him dearly, but the second the word's out of his mouth, he's already begun to dig into the spinach soufflé that's on his plate next to the broiled whitefish.

"How're things?" he adds.

Before I answer, he's returned to eating with a vengeance.

He doesn't mean to be like that. It happens.

He's a clinician with a fine office on North Michigan Avenue. His approach to psychotherapy is, to use his own word, "eclectic." He does marriage counseling, group and individual therapy, behavior mod, and even, on occasion, hypnosis to cure alcoholics and obese people, though he's actually never come right out and said he would like to put me under.

If my mother, who sits at the other end of our elliptical dining room table, is correct, he's not at his best when he's hungry.

Between the two of them, in the center of the table, there's a colorful splash of fresh flowers, so that their views of each other are obstructed.

To my father's right—always—sits eight-year-old Matthew.

To my father's left—at least until she decides to go off to college—sits Heather.

Since I always sit to Heather's left, I always stare across the table into nothingness.

It *is* true that I sit to my mother's right, but sitting next to her feels like being in a bell jar, even though I love and admire her, too.

Her reaction to my greeting is subtler—if that's possible—than my father's.

"Hi," she says. Period.

Staring into that nothingness opposite me but so utterly famished that I plunge right into the spinach soufflé, I throw caution to the wind and say, with my mouth full, "Dr. Rogers is starting a block honors program for *twenty*—ahem!—twenty students out of the entire Livingston sophomore class beginning after Christmas."

I don my undaunted look, the shoveling down of my food notwithstanding.

I've told no one in the entire world about this invitation from the only teacher in my life I have ever idolized. Or adored, whichever.

When there's no immediate reaction, I toss in, "He's asked me to be one of the twenty, and I've said yes."

Understand what's going on here.

For nearly three hours at Wardman's Merchandise Center, I have stored within me a blossoming self-esteem I thought had been reserved for normal human beings only.

Not for underachieving middle children.

But now what? I'm in my *own* home, a place—right?—that ought to connote love and kindness and empathy? Particularly with parents who are, respectively, a psychologist and a sociologist?

And what do I hear?

Nothing!

Zilch!

Heather looks up from her plate and startles me by saying, "Didn't Dr. Rogers just begin to teach English at Livingston when I was in my first or second year there? The Livingston administration can't take an honors program seriously if it's entrusting it to such a junior member of the English department. I'd have thought Cynthia Bialek and he—"

"What?" I say, as ravenous for gossip as for food.

"Nothing," she says. "I was just confusing something."

What's she got up her sleeve?

My hands go right for my weak spot, the thighs. I squeeze them into the tiniest masses the laws of the universe will allow, thereby firing arrows of pain straight up to my brain.

What I wouldn't do to have Heather's thighs.

As much as I love her, though, what I'd like to tell her right now is, "Heather, darling, go suck on a lemon if you're going to dangle your superior knowledge in front of me when it's my story."

As it is, I give her the eye.

We continue eating in silence, interrupted only by the clinking of forks and knives against plates and Matthew's slurping of his milk.

When my father's scraped his plate clean, he says, "I think that's great, Hope. Seriously."

"Thanks, Dad," I say. Better late than never, right?

Then Matthew, whom I've yet to beat at chess, wipes his mouth with the back of his hand—much to our mother's chagrin—and says, "Is a block honors program for blockheads?"

For a brat, he's got an enviable sense of humor.

Still, the simple fact is that because of Dr. Everett Rogers, I should be entitled for once to unadulterated exhilaration.

And I'll be darned if I'm going to let a comedian spoil it!

Or a sister who keeps secrets!

Etiquette or not, I stick my tongue out at both of them. I'd rather be a little more demonstrative, actually, but this is dinner, after all.

If that man will have me, I'm thinking as Heather, Matthew, and I begin our cleanup chores, *I'll be-*

come one of those leaders of the twenty-first century he's designed his program for.

Think of it!

A *female* critical thinker whom the sexists and chauvinists of the world *will* listen to and take note of and not do everything in their power to poke fun at!

When I go upstairs to my bedroom afterward and take a look at myself in the mirror, however, the roller coaster dips sharply.

Doubt besieges me.

Can a blah like me do it?

Oh, Dr. Rogers, pray!

3

FRIDAY MORNING, I try to forget my dread of having to do wind sprints in PE by fantasizing about the program and the Sophomore Cotillion, held in the spring at the Women's Club downtown.

To overcome the absurdity of my appearance in a gym suit, I imagine myself in this . . . well, almost . . . slinky red chiffon gown, slit the length of each gorgeous thigh, hanging on to the tuxedoed arm of the nicest guy—Lord, I hope there is one!—in the honors program, maybe six feet tall and utterly compassionate.

Not, of course, that there'd be a snowball's chance that anybody with sense would ask or that I'd have the nerve to ask someone.

"C'mon, Gallagher," Ms. Slender Perfecto Philbon, our PE teacher, screams. "Pay attention. These sprints are for record." That's, of course, what she *says*, but what she's thinking is, *C'mon, fatso! Move your butt!*

She's got her silver stopwatch in her hand. Her legs—in these bright-red-with-gold-stripe spandex pants—straddle the yellow line on the gleaming floor, and she looks like one of your Olympic medalists, an indecent ten in everything!

The whole blasted class's watching me by now, of course!

But all I can see is the opposite end of the gym, which has to be a good mile off. All I can hear is her shriek, "Go!"

Maybe, I muse to the thunderous thump of my heart, *Dr. Rogers'll come to the cotillion with his wife. Yes! That's it! He'll tap the six-footer's shoulder and ask, "Would you mind if I had this dance with Ms. Gallagher? With Hope?"*

I lurch at the "Go!"

A knife's stabbing me right through the chest.

My cheeks burn.

Darn my legs! Like anchors, they pull first one side of me, then the other down toward the horrible, ugly, beastly floor.

What's that?

Jeers and hoots and howls?

Converging on me like thundering boulders in an avalanche?

I'll die, that's what, before I flop on my face in front of them all!

Die!

I'm going to be a twenty-first-century leader, right, Dr. Rogers?

You promised!

Yes!

But oh, Lord, in the meanwhile, give me air!

Don't let me faint!

Let me live long enough to train for my new role!

Everything before me blurs in salty, searing images of humiliation.

My body, with a will of its own, hurtles me into this endless tunnel of derision toward the horses at the far end of the gym.

"You're going to have to pick up some speed there, Gallagher," Philbon's voice, like a rumbling, tumbling echo, cajoles me as I collide with the horse. I drip with perspiration, my limbs numb and detached, lying back there somewhere behind me on the ignominious (thanks for the new word, Dr. Rogers!) gym floor.

Ecstatic that the ordeal's finally over, I rush through the shower—I'll be taking another before going to bed tonight anyway, so why bother now?—and then make my way to English.

In this, the last honors English class before vacation, we're to discuss John Updike's story "A & P," and how rites of passage, to be meaningful, always have to entail painful choices.

I sink with considerable relief into my seat.

My heart's still leaping through my chest from the stupid sprint, but now that I'm here, I don't care.

In *his* classroom, serenity and joy reign.

Dr. Rogers asks, "What change does Sammy undergo?" It's a question I expected he would ask, having become, over the last couple of months, attuned to his educational approach.

Joshua Melamed raises his hand, and when Dr. Rogers, color uncoordinated as usual but irresistible anyway, when Dr. Rogers acknowledges him, Joshua responds. "Fro . . . from . . . er . . . um . . . trea . . . treating girls . . . er . . . like . . . like sex objects to respecting them as . . . uh . . . sensitive, feeling human beings?" Since he's had a chance to become comfortable in this class, Joshua's stutter is no longer terribly pronounced.

Whether his answer's right or wrong is beside the point. Just from listening to it and to the way Joshua presents it, not pushy or anything but in the form of a question, you can tell immediately that here's one completely modest whiz who doesn't care two whits if someone notices him or not.

"Fine, Mr. Melamed," Dr. Rogers says.

As he told us right in the beginning of the course, he uses the formal mode of address when he calls on us "in deference to your being adults now and therefore deserving titles of respect and dignity."

"Fine, indeed," he repeats. "But you've stolen my show. You've left me with little more to say because you're exactly right. Sammy, in Updike's story, goes from being a typical sexist male who uses words like 'can' and 'fuselage' to describe parts of female and male anatomy, respectively, to a caring, compassionate, empathetic individual who can't live with his boss Lengel's simplistic notion that being 'decently dressed' is the same as being a 'decent' human being."

Dr. Rogers slides off the edge of his desk, walks around to the blackboard, and draws a straight line, labeling it A at one end and, five or six feet farther along, Z at the other, adding a series of vees to the line a foot or so apart, like arrowheads.

"If," he says, "our lives are like this line and each crisis we encounter is like one of these vees, so that, in each crisis, we have a minimum of at least two ways to go, then Sammy unconsciously, in this story, opts for the more difficult route."

Gym and sweat and ignominy are, by now, a trillion miles away.

A wrinkle at the back of his jacket, a chilling scratch from the chalk he wields, the soft brush of his shoes against the floor as he unthinkingly, spontaneously moves to make his marks—each and all, like magnets, pull me out of myself into his body, his arms, his head.

It amazes me that both Dr. Rogers and Joshua have been able to get so much out of the Updike story. All I saw, at first reading anyway, was that Sammy changed, yes, but not *that* significantly.

Lord!

What follows is this intense class dialogue. Socratic, Dr. Rogers likes to call it. Because he makes everyone get involved somehow or other, asking questions he really knows the answers to but that he wants us to pull out of *ourselves*, as though they were inside us all the while, simply waiting for a little prod.

I'm absolutely dying to rush up to him and ask when and where the new block program will meet. But, of course, no matter how impulsive I may be, even *I* know the timing's wrong.

When the bell rings, he wishes us happy holidays and winks that wink of his that inevitably tears me apart.

We get up to go.

But I can't resist.

By a series of dexterous maneuvers, I manage to be at the tail end of the students leaving the room.

I cough out an ahem.

"Ms. Gallagher," Dr. Rogers says—as I thought he might. "Why is it I'm getting a feeling that you want to speak to me?"

He talks that way—sort of unintimidatingly—so that you not only have no choice but to speak, you feel that if you don't he'll be terribly disappointed.

"Uh . . . er . . . yessir," I blunder on. "I, uh, know it's . . . er . . . um . . . presumptuous of me . . ."

"Something about the new program, right?" he says, the teal blue of his eyes like whirlpools sucking me into my destiny.

"Yes . . . well . . . but, Dr. Rogers, sir . . ."

"Anything you want to know, Ms. Gallagher," he says, "you just ask."

When has a teacher ever, ever invited you to feel free to ask about anything?

"Uh . . . where . . . that is, sir . . . when and how . . ."

He beckons me—a first-class stumbling, bumbling idiot—to follow him out of the room, talking as we go.

"There'll be an orientation, first day back from vacation," he says, reading my mind like the genius he is.

I work a little at my ability to smile.

Then, marking a first for me anyway, I dare to say as I leave him, "I can't wait, sir."

And the truth is, I really can't.

DURING CHRISTMAS BREAK, I'm ebullient . . . until an incident at Wardman's one afternoon just before New Year's.

The merchandise center's been teeming with people every hour of every day until the place's like an insane asylum. Customers of all ages ricochet off one another. Helter-skelter, they grab stuff from the shelves or jam it back in where it doesn't belong, not troubled at all by the electronic eyes all over the place.

Every hour on the hour, Danny Stewart's lion voice bellows out from his den on the mezzanine, just to the right of the ten registers, "Hourly cash receipts!"

It's a command not to be dealt with lightly. Wardman's doesn't take kindly to shortages at the end of a shift. I know, from the personal experience of being short twenty dollars once and having to live that week with a twenty-dollar-smaller paycheck.

So I'm trying hard to do things right. Granted, that might not be great in an absolute sense. But for me, it's a lot.

Danny's crass ineloquence, each and every hour, sends the trembles through me.

At the four o'clock bellow, I am about to ring up a sale for this . . . well . . . slim and beautiful girl from Livingston. I have seen and envied her countless times at school—who wouldn't, her being either a size three or five? She, clearly, has *never* noticed me unless it's because *I'm* somewhere around an eleven or thirteen, depending on the cut, and how could you avoid spotting that?

Instead of ringing her up *first* and *then* clearing the register for my four o'clock reading, which is what I would normally do, Danny's roar and her appearance addle me and I clear the *register* first and let *her* wait.

What comes next is fuzzy to me, it happens so fast, but I do believe she, with her tons of eye shadow and eyebrow pencil and mascara and foundation, gives me the finger in front of the whole world. Stunned, I, at one and the same time, return the favor and say, "That isn't nice, you know," and add *her* sale to the hourly reading accidentally, which I then tear off and hand her.

I can't believe what I've done.

She goes bonkers!

"What the hell you doin'?" she cries out, her hands with their purple fingernails planted on the sliver of her waist.

If I could shrivel up now, I would.

But there isn't time.

Danny Stewart comes rushing over to my register so fast, I haven't got time to turn red.

He's gnashing his teeth and arching his eyebrows a mile a minute.

You'd think there'd been an earthquake and everyone and her mother was screaming for help.

The knot in me crushes its way up through my throat.

Danny doesn't say as much as boo.

Suddenly, he turns on this oily smile at what's her name—Madonna?—and titters, "Don'tcha go worryin' there, miss. I'm gonna straighten this here out [he gives my knees this glare!] in a jiffy," and begins to punch keys on the register and check the tape and ring up more keys.

By the time he's through, I've buckled. As soon as she leaves, he'll give me the "pink slip" look he's famous for, and I'll probably be jobless. I know it!

And . . . and Miss Finger-happy there, I'll bet, will go back to Livingston after Christmas and start rumors guaranteed to deter any sensible sophomore from ever asking me to the Spring Cotillion.

I can hear her now.

"Ya know that tub someone spilled into size thirteen jeans so's they're splittin' at the seams and her knock-knees are stickin' out? Would ya believe what she done to me at Wardman's during vacation?"

Greater catastrophes have occurred over less!

So I steel myself, pressing up tight against the ledge to the right of the register to give Danny Stewart all the leeway he wants.

He still doesn't say anything to me, though I can hear him in my head roaring, "Damn it, Hope Gallagher. Don'tcha know better?" Or, "Gallagher! You're even stupider'n I thought, which is plenty, lemme tell ya!"

He says to mascaraed "Madonna" again, "Sorry, there . . . uh . . . for the—d'ya know what I'm sayin'?—inconvenience, ma'am," as if she were Princess Di or someone.

He hands her a new receipt, fidgets with the register, takes a close look at the tape he's punched out.

And she wiggles off with this smug toss of her dyed blonde hair, among other parts of her anatomy.

Then he signals to an older gentleman who is next in line to wait just a moment, and fiddles a little more with the keys of the register.

When he thinks no one's listening, he gargles out

a whisper to me, "Watch it, Gallagher. I'm just tellin' you to watch it."

He has said it so softly, my brain tells me no one could conceivably have heard.

But that's my brain.

My spastic colon's beating out a message to the knot in my throat that my days at Wardman's are numbered.

So that by the time Danny Stewart's returned to his spying tower up in the mezzanine, I'm all thumbs with the older gentleman, fumbling with his items like a neophyte, for God's sake, instead of like a four-month veteran checker-outer.

How can I function in an honors program?

All at once, the ebullience that was, isn't.

Poof!

Like that.

Slogging my way home through the falling snow that alights on my nose and cheeks and lips, I wish I could reach Dr. Rogers and tell him, "It won't work, sir. Thanks for the compliment, but can't you see you've picked a loser?"

But there's no way for me to reach him.

Which means I'm doomed to fail before his very eyes when school resumes.

Who knows?

Maybe I won't get past the first day!

5

HEATHER, to her credit, picks up on the difference in me New Year's Eve day as she passes my room. She is on her way to a friend's house.

I am propped up against my hypoallergenic pillows, thumbing through Sylvia Plath's poetry, looking for "Tulips," which is morbid enough to fit my mood to a tee.

Heather plants herself in the doorway, dressed in her stunning new cable-knit sweater and plaid skirt, which, of course, she can afford to wear because *her* legs are perfect.

I still haven't forgiven her for belittling Dr. Rogers and then, adding injury to insult, dropping Cynthia Bialek's name like that.

"What's wrong?" she says.

My God! I'm thinking. *Does it show that much?* I fiddle with my split ends.

"Oh," I say, "nothing." I don't want her to think the mention of Dr. Rogers and Bialek awhile back has piqued my curiosity, which of course it has.

Though she hasn't made up her mind yet about college, she's got a lot of sensitivity for a nineteen-year-old, even though the two of us haven't been what you'd call really close.

The distance between us has nothing to do with her being a size six either!

Not at all.

We just haven't been terribly close, that's all, whether because she and Matthew are and always have been honors students and I haven't, who knows?

I swing my legs over the side of the bed farthest from her.

That yearning to call Dr. Rogers to tell him I should withdraw surfaces again, and I turn my face away from Heather.

Why should I give her the satisfaction of seeing me on the verge of tears?

She says in a laid-back tone of voice, "Want to talk about it?"

My bedroom's square, with this white shag rug to the left of the bed. A foot from the rug is this white-enameled rolltop desk my father and my mother got for me years ago.

The minute she asks, the room feels like a cage that's locked.

It's not easy for me to take, her being concerned like this.

I stand up and meander over to the bookcase, as though the world's my oyster, and take out the copy of Laura Ingalls Wilder's *Little House in the Big Woods*, which the folks started reading to me when I was maybe this big and for which I will forever thank them. Holding it in my hands brings back tons of memories of how life used to be for human beings in the old days, so what have I got to complain about?

Riffling through the pages, my back toward her, I present this stiff upper torso so she'll think things are ginger peachy.

But she's breathing down my neck!

"Hey, c'mon, Hope!" she says. "What's a sister for?"

God, if that doesn't top everything!

"Okay, already," I mumble, afraid my voice's going to crack. "Okay."

I can feel her cable-knit sweater on my arm.

Her hand reaches for mine.

All inside, I start to crumble!

In the little bit of natural light coming in through the blinds, her hair shimmers.

"Come on," she pleads. "Two heads sometimes are better than one."

That does it!

I spin around.

Powee!

There I go, obesity personified, flopping all over her, my head buried in her shoulder, gurgling like a two-year-old!

Can you believe it!

Gurgling! Sobbing!

And over what, Lord Almighty!

A crazy job!

Getting a rotten finger!

Knowing I'm going to fail the first day I'm in *his* class!

"Sssh," Heather says. "It's going to be okay."

You can bet anything, some sisters in her position, firstborn and all, might not give me the time of day.

After all, she's got her own problems, don'tcha think?

But I just have to get one peek at her eyes and I know she means it.

Does she ever mean it!

So I tell her what happened at Wardman's.

I tell her about my doubts about the program.

She pulls me down onto the bed by her side.

"Want to know something?" she says. "When I made that crack about Dr. Rogers being junior, it was a not too clever way of covering up *my* jealousy."

Who'd ever have believed it?

Still, she's not saying a word about Dr. Bialek.

"You're in that program because you're so darn bright, don't you know, Hope? And as far as what happened at Wardman's, well . . . I went to school with Danny Stewart, so enough said on that account. He'll still be checking registers long after you've gone on and made all of us here proud of your achievements."

Talk about goose bumps!

I've begun to levitate!

I hug her so tight, I can't remember the last time I hugged anybody that way. Why . . . why . . . we rise up, up into this gloriously warm expanse of . . . of—what would you call it?—spring water, clear and pure, pristine and buoyant, where all bodies are created equal.

It's the most glorious feeling a person can have!

I shriek out, "Heather, you're the *best*!"

The two of us turn maudlin simultaneously.

"I," she says, "beg to differ with you. *You*'re the best. And I'm really happy you're in that program."

The ebullience returns, and I feel ready to take on the world.

6

WHEN SCHOOL resumes after Christmas, I find myself sitting agog, surrounded by brilliant people in the conference room.

It's the group's first meeting, and except for Dr. Rogers and Joshua Melamed, I know no one.

Me? With all these geniuses?

Can't be!

Twenty of us share a table with—*with*, mind you!—Dr. Cynthia Bialek, philosophy (about whom, I confess, I don't know what to think, she's staring at Dr. Rogers so peculiarly); Mrs. Laura Courtney, biology; Mr. Harold Leventhal, mathematics; Dr. Larry Haggerty, history; Mr. Sloan, head of counseling—as though we are, Lord Almighty, their peers.

It's terrifying!

I shudder with fear that at any instant one or some or all of them will turn to me with pointed fingers and, en masse, scream out, "There's the airhead! Get rid of her!"

And, of course, standing statuesquely at the long blackboard, wearing his broadly checked sport jacket and loud tie, is Dr. Everett Rogers.

He and the other faculty get little pieces of picayune mechanics out of the way, like how the group can use the conference room in the Levian Wing near Dr. Rogers's office on the second floor as its home base, a place to congregate and chew the—ugh!—*fat*.

When Dr. Rogers calls roll, it sounds like a United Nations: Anderson, Arzawa, Bernstein, Chomolieski, Gallagher, Goodman, Guitterez, Helipoulous, Hussein, Jones, McLaughlin, Meier, Melamed, Nguyen, O'Hara, Roosevelt, Swetchkov, Untermeyer, Valenti, Welch.

I turn all ears the moment he—with that voice of his that is like the sound of a violin when the violinist's bow is arcing its way across the strings in an intricate maneuver—the moment that Dr. Rogers opens the seminar with his introductory lecture.

"From Ptolemy and geocentrism to Copernicus and heliocentrism; from anthropomorphism to Darwinism and human beings evolving from monkeys; from Godhead to God is dead; ideology and principle to Id and maggotry; from hero to anti-hero . . ."

I begin to get goose bumpy; perhaps I'll die on the spot? For nearly fifteen years, what have I done but build up this resentment toward schools and teachers? Beginning as early as the second grade, when Mrs. Ragan asked everyone in class to give their address, and so I did—5555 South Sandal-wood Drive. And right there, in front of everyone, she called me a liar—only a fool would believe a person's address would have four fives in it! So I, of course, immediately decided to wait for Heather after school, who was supposed to walk me home every day anyway, being my elder, and when she came I asked her what her girlfriend Cindy's address was, and she told me—didn't I know?—Cindy and her family had just moved to Highland Park. But I didn't care where she had moved to. Wouldn't she, Heather, please write Cindy's address down on a piece of paper in her very best handwriting? Which she did. Thirty-three fourteen Cedar Lane, High-land Park. And that address, in what I believed to be Heather's finest handwriting, I handed to Mrs. Ragan the next morning and then slithered to my seat, thrilling, in the meantime, in delicious victory. Until Mrs. Ragan's razor-edged voice cut through the chitter-chatter of second graders settling down: "Hope Gallagher, you are apparently a pathological liar. Come here right now! It simply isn't possible for *you* to live in Highland Park and go to school in Chicago! You live in Chicago, not Highland Park!"

Talk about no-win situations!

But now!

Now!

His words are like musical notes soaring from a Stradivarius.

He and the words, the words and the ideas, become one.

One.

Indivisible.

Incarnate.

I can't stop shaking.

All at once, finally, at last, after fifteen years, I've begun to learn. From his brain and body to my brain and body, the only kind of real communication has taken place—an invisible transportation. I know without knowing exactly, precisely, immediately what he means by Ptolemy and geocentrism and Copernicus and heliocentrism.

Don't ask me when, where, how I learned the names and concepts, but it's as though they've been lying dormant in my head since before birth! The music of language now, like some precious, some mysterious, and long-lost key, has found its way to my lock and opened me up to everything.

A minute before, had you asked me to define *anthropomorphism*, I would have said, "Go suck on a lemon! How should I know?"

Now, though, it's as clear to me as if I were still

living among the ancient Greeks and shaping the gods into human forms.

Shocks of electricity zip and zap to all parts of my skin.

As I prop my chin into the palms of my hands to concentrate more intently—so as not to miss a single syllable or the minusculest of his breaths—his teal blue eyes grow large and seem to take in the entire universe. Not just this tiny room or the relatively few of us mortals Fate has granted the good fortune to put at his revered feet.

"What people have called progress," he says, "and the rise of civilization have brought us to this present moment when, if a thing can be done, we do it. We can build a Sears Tower. Do you want one? Then let us build it. Once, however, before industrialization and high technology contributed to our dehumanization, once we might have asked, Even if we *can* build a Sears Tower, the real question is, should we?"

His words pass from him to me, and I am infected.

I tremble with his contagious disease.

Our Victorian house on Sandalwood Drive—with all its rehabbed exterior that obviates (he taught me that!) its ever having to be painted again (*ever!*)—leaps before my eyes. All three stories of it, so divided that, as my father once put it, "each of us could be separate and equal and have his or her own space." Why did my father not *once* consider the possibility that *separation* leads to *alienation*?

Maybe if the five of us had been more squashed together physically, I wouldn't have ended up being such an airhead.

"What I guess I'm trying to say, ladies and gentlemen," Dr. Rogers continues, "is that this program, I hope, in its multidisciplinary approach toward a unified concern for the salvation of mankind in the twenty-first—"

He has begun to pull his chair from the table in preparation to take his seat.

There is the faintest hint of a kind of sadness in the sagging line of his lips, as if he almost wishes it hadn't all come to this, the need for an honors program; that perhaps, maybe, he wishes it hadn't become necessary to pass on to the twenty of us the flickering torch of a dying or dead way of life. It's as though he'd like to say that we don't have a heck of a lot of time—just two more years, if the program succeeds—before we go out into an automated world of people dizzy on computers and cellular phones and VCRs.

But with one hand clasping the chair top and with the other in the air seemingly trying to pull the word "century" from his mouth—frozen like that in mid-thought, Dr. Everett Rogers's spell is rent by this thunderclap that explodes from Dr. Bialek.

"Please," she shrieks. "Don't be sexist and chauvinistic in *this* program. In this program least of all.

Maybe you could get away with that machismo voodooism once in private, damn it! But not here! Not now! Have the decency and intelligence to speak of *human*kind when you're in public. That crap about 'anthropomorphism' is hypocritical. You've laid that trip on us from the beginning of time! Gods in the shape of men, my foot!"

I can't believe it!

The magnitude of the shriek!

The thought *There is something between them!* makes me flinch.

I don't dare look up at *anyone*, but I can feel in my bones that everyone else's been traumatized, too.

A pall, like dirt being heaved onto a coffin, settles over the room.

A palpable dread of more to come surrounds us.

Dr. Rogers, bent at the waist over the chair, gropes first one way, then another for a place to go.

Suddenly, in his broad-checked jacket and loud tie, tall and lean as he is, with his lips still parted as though the word "century" is stuck and so he can't close them—suddenly, the picture of him frozen there like that stirs me to want to rush to his side.

But Mr. Sloan, the counselor in the program, stands up and says, "Time for this first seminar is up, people. We'll see you in the regular courses of the program beginning tomorrow morning."

Dr. Rogers puts his notes in a manila folder and erases the blackboard. Barely audibly, he says,

"Will you please pick up this handout on the desk, Erik Erikson's 'The Golden Rule in the Light of New Insight,' and read it for next time?"

Mr. Sloan, Mr. Leventhal, Dr. Haggerty, and Dr. Bialek leave, the last like a tornado wreaking havoc at one hundred fifty miles per.

Mrs. Courtney, a small, delicate woman, stops just as she nears him, as though she wants to say something to Dr. Rogers.

But then you can see her shaking her head; she'd like to say something, but—God!—what's to say?

As always, I'm at the tail end of the students filing out into the hallway.

Oh, Lord, I'm thinking. *If only . . . if only I could . . . would I like . . .*

But I haven't the foggiest notion in the world what I would or what I could do—except, maybe, get hold of Heather right away and press at her till she tells me something about Dr. Bialek. But if Dr. Rogers thinks I'm impulsive now, that'd only reinforce him.

So, drenched, I pick up the thick handout and store this moment of his humiliation in that part of me where vengeance reigns.

7

A GIRL whose name Dr. Rogers called after mine when he took attendance, Rosa Guitterez, stops me and several others after the orientation fiasco and says, "Please, would you all like to go to Mooky's for a snack?"

She's a little thing, with sparkling dark eyes and lovely short black hair.

Levians teem up and down the hallway in every conceivable state of attire and appearance. Many are decked out in orange, purple, and yellow punk hairdos, *nose rings* as well as *quadruple* earrings, tight leather slacks and jackets.

Though none of us knows the others—except for Joshua Melamed and me—Dr. Bialek's outburst has bound our small group together into a tiny clump in the hallway like survivors on a lifeboat.

It doesn't take more than a minute for some of us to agree that Mooky's, which I've never been to but which I've heard about, would be a fabulous idea just about now.

Someone who identifies herself as Tamara Goodman—I can see immediately *I* will identify with her, taking a quick measure of the circumference of *her* thighs—wonders aloud, "Are we allowed to do that, go out of the school building this early in the day without permission?"

The guy who's introduced himself as Tommy Anderson and who looks like a basketball player says, "I'm pretty sure we can."

So seven of us—Rosa Guitterez, Tamara Goodman, Joshua Melamed, Tommy Anderson, Doreen McLaughlin, Tuy Nguyen (I'm not sure how to pronounce his name), and I—arrange to meet at Mooky's after we've gotten our coats from our lockers.

The place is relatively empty when we get there, and led by Tommy Anderson, we head over to a booth way in the back.

Mooky himself—I'm guessing that's who it is from his commanding presence—comes to take our orders—french fries and Cokes—and then Rosa, in a high-pitched voice that has a crisp edge to it, says, "I wish to tell all of you"—she eyes her boots—"Dr. Bialek's my homeroom teacher. Please do not read anything into her. . . ."

You can tell that she comes from a proper home, where family members who want something at the dinner table exercise gentility in making their requests: "Would you kindly pass me this, Mother?" "Would you kindly pass me that, Father?"

I love it!

I'd like to put my two cents in and add, "Bialek's not *my* homeroom teacher, but I'll bet my sister Heather knows a thing or two about her." I'm not about, however, to make opening remarks yet in a group like this, especially when what's at stake here, dear Lord, are the intimacies of my . . . that is, of people's lives!

Joshua's sitting to the right of me, wearing a gray parka. The greenish white fluorescents from overhead glint off his thick glasses.

"But . . . but . . . but . . . a . . . a . . . Ros . . . Rosa . . ." He stutters, not yet comfortable in this *new* group. "Sh . . . e . . . she . . . Bia . . . Bial . . . Bialek . . . sh . . . shou . . . shouldn't . . . shouldn't . . ."

We hardly know each other, Joshua and me, but I can't tell you how proud I am of him right now, getting right to the heart of our depression as he's trying to do.

Rosa goes on.

"I just wish . . . what Dr. Bialek said in the seminar . . ." she says. "Please try to understand her. It's her way. She's not as she sounds, I swear to you. What she said, perhaps, means nothing."

The Vietnamese or Korean boy, who's sitting at the booth in a chair that's in the aisle, says, "My name is Tuy Nguyen." A timid smile spreads across his lips. He stares at his hands on his lap. "Though it is spelled T-U-Y N-G-U-Y-E-N, it is pronounced TIE WIN." He looks around the table now with a hint of mischievousness in his eyes. "In sports, as you can see, my name would be—I believe it is the right word to use here—a paradox, since if one merely 'ties' a game, one cannot simultaneously 'win' it."

His hair gleams black, and his deep-set eyes, from behind metal-framed glasses, see right into you, when he can work up the courage to overcome his obvious modesty and look at you directly.

"But if you will permit me, I have heard Dr.—is it BY-YEL-EK or BEE-YAH-LEK?—Dr. Bialek is—how do you say?—aggressive?"

Because I've heard Heather pronounce the name before, now I *do* put my two cents in: "It's pronounced BEE-YAH-LEK," I say.

To myself, I'm repeating *his* name to get *it* right: TIE WIN, TIE WIN, TIE WIN.

Rosa darts in. "She's a very brilliant woman who can teach us much. She's eager to get the most out of one and can sound harsh. Please . . . I wish you would all . . . yes . . . forgive her." She's dodging again—as maybe Heather did, too!—the sexual im-plications of Bialek's behavior.

Across the way from me, the auburn-haired girl, Doreen McLaughlin, waves her angora-sweatered arm for attention.

"My friends call me Doty, not Doreen, so I wish you all would, too. Mrs. Courtney, whom I abso-lutely adore, recommended me for the program, so I'm happy to meet all of you. Really."

She straightens one side of her waist-long hair until it just about kills me with envy.

"I don't think Dr. Bialek should have said what she said to him in front of all of us, either, but who knows what *he* said to deserve it, d'ya know what I mean? But, like I said, Mrs. Courtney recom-mended me and I think like well maybe we've all got the chance of a lifetime here. And maybe even the teachers are nervous this first day, do you see what I'm saying, so why don't we listen to Rosa here and forgive and forget?"

Their conversation converges on me all at once in this horrendously explosive headache. I can't hold it in another second, whether I'm frightened to death among geniuses like these or not.

"Dr. Rogers," I say, "is the finest teacher at Liv-ingston High. He *didn't* mean anything sex-ist"—before I can check it, it comes out anyway—"or sexual when he used the word 'man-kind.' It's crazy for anyone to think so."

Immediately, I shrink in shame behind Joshua.

If Dr. Rogers were sexist, would he want to prepare me and the others here—females or not—to be leaders of the twenty-first century, for heaven's sake? And if there were anything sexual between . . . God, I can't even think it!

"That's what I've heard, too," Tommy Anderson offers. "I mean, a lot of teachers—especially in honors programs—have this bias against, say, jocks, but when Mr. Leventhal recommended me, Dr. Rogers didn't hesitate at all. So he's sure okay in my book."

As we're eating, Tuy Nguyen (TIE WIN! TIE WIN!) says, wiping catsup from his lips, "I will reserve judgment, then, about Dr. BEE-YAH-LEK, for if such a teacher as you say Dr. Rogers is chose her for the honors program, her behavior today should be forgiven as Rosa has said. She surely must have her reasons."

He glances my way, his eyes warm and pleading.

Could he know whatever it is that Heather knows?

Doty thrusts her hand, palm up, to the center of the table, and one by one the rest of us, like volleyball team players, heap our palms on top of hers.

The feeling's *nearly* terrific!

Tommy Anderson says, "Mr. Sloan said the program starts tomorrow, so I'd suggest we meet at someone's house tonight to discuss Dr. Rogers's handout. It's a foot thick."

I'm wishing, *Maybe Tuy Nguyen'll offer.*

But Doty rushes in. "You're all welcome at my place after dinner."

I tell them about working at Wardman's.

Tuy says, "For Hope Gallagher's sake, then, I suggest we meet at your home at a time convenient to her."

Everyone agrees.

Talk about the New Year getting off to an auspicious start!

THE NEXT DAY, Dr. Rogers, wearing a, for him, somber blue blazer against an aqua shirt and striped red tie, explains that his class in the program will concentrate on critical reading, thinking, and writing.

He has entered the classroom stiffly, his thin lips clenched, his jawbone twitching.

From my seat in the front row—the first time I've ever of my own volition chosen to sit directly *this* close to a teacher—I intuit dreadful vibrations emanating from the depths of his soul.

I fear for his life.

Still, in addition to his handout yesterday, he now distributes a long reading list.

You can tell he wants to put us at ease by injecting a note of humor in the observation "Please don't any of you let the length of the list, or the difficulty of the Erikson piece, frighten you. I'm simply trying to impress you, that's all."

The others laugh.

But for me, anyway, his effort fails.

I can *hear* his heart thumping!

With the kind of courage that makes an imbecile like me flinch with envy, he sits down on the corner of his desk as though he hadn't a worry in the world, the Bialek rhubarb being mere trivia, and begins.

"What?" he says. "What new insight?"

Let me be honest right up front.

I counted the pages of the Erikson essay before I began to read it, a habit I picked up early in my educational life from those teachers who unconsciously force you to think numbers only.

Despite the group's going to Doty's last night and *sort* of trying to poke through it, the essay is unbelievably long and incredibly obtuse, to put it mildly.

The print is minuscule. Single-spaced, two columns to a page.

But for Dr. Rogers . . . well . . . I'd do anything. Nearly.

I couldn't and wouldn't ask my father, who has bandied the name Erikson about the house over the years, to give me one iota's worth of help on this one.

Which meant spending three more hours, after discussion with the group last night, yellow-markering the handout on my own until it now looks like a neon wilderness.

And not understanding much of it at all, *not at all*. . . .

Though I now wish I were my more normal invisible self in the back row, the fact of the matter is that here I am, under Dr. Rogers's nose. I'm accumulating perspiration at the small of my back at an incredible rate and in unbelievable quantities, and experiencing pangs of shame over my stupidity. Simultaneously, on the other hand, I'm taking in peripherally the shadows on Dr. Rogers's face that today have lengthened to the ridges of his cheekbones.

Is he a role model of courage or what?

Lord, give me this man's strength!

For him to be able to go on as if Bialek never . . . Well!

The silence following his question grows to such intensity, it kills slowly.

I pray that good old Joshua Melamed will come to the rescue. If not him, Rosa Guitterez or Tamara Goodman. Or . . . Tuy Nguyen (TIE WIN, idiot! TIE WIN!).

When Joshua doesn't say a word, I inhale a whopper of a breath and cover my knee holes with the handout, yellow-markered side up and visible.

I flash this moronic smile at Dr. Rogers. This should convince him what a terrible mistake he's made, picking a computer glitch if ever there was one for this program.

Dr. Rogers takes another stab.

"What new insight?" he says, squirming. "And why? Why does Erikson choose to look at the ancient Golden Rule: Do unto others as you would have them do unto you. Why suddenly try to gain a new insight into a rule that has seemed to serve us so well for millennia?"

An awful, wrenching, nauseating queasiness creeps over me.

The silence deafens.

I cross my legs and plead, *You guys are the geniuses! Answer the man!*

Suddenly, thank the Lord, a voice.

"The advent of the Atomic Age."

Unmistakably, it's Tuy Nguyen.

In his metal-framed glasses, he makes no fashion or political statement. He couldn't care less what other people think about him or the glasses or the two together.

What has to be has to be.

Dr. Rogers's mouth opens and the voice tremulates again. The response seems to have brought him back to his old self.

"Perfect, Mr. Nguyen," he says, using the formal mode of address in his usual fashion.

"And . . . and . . ." He treads gently now, so as not to disturb the fine-tuned equilibrium of twenty souls at the edges of their seats who might, with just a single wrong word, be lost forever. "And what role does Erikson's use of Gandhi in the essay play to support Mr. Nguyen's claim?"

His teal blue eyes, softened only slightly by the deepening shadows brought on by the attack of you know who, alight on—of all people—me.

I'm a goner!

If you have ever walked a tightrope for the first time in your life, you will understand what those eyes, which I have come to love to the very pit of my soul, are doing to me. At the high altitude of a tightrope and with no prior experience in such endeavors, a person shudders in subtle wafts of winds on the way to purgatory.

Flabbergasted?

Petrified?

Intimidated?

Try paralyzed.

Try hyperventilating and stupefied.

Incredulous and astonished; colicky and panicky.

If I've said it once, I've said it a thousand times.

The man's words, his *breaths*, dear Lord, become knowledge incarnate, transported by what act of God I do not know from the innards of his cerebellum to the innards of mine by vibrations so ultra-invisible and otherwise undetectable, they land on me—his words and thoughts and breaths do—as though they had never left him.

From some mysterious portion of me, an area of my being I did not know I had—because certainly I do not, absolutely, positively do not remember reading or underlining it—flows a statement in the very same musical rhythms I have learned to identify as his and his alone.

The words reach my lips and depart therefrom, and *I* can even hear them, but I do not for a moment believe they can possibly be coming from me.

" 'That line of action alone is justice that does not do harm to either party to a dispute,' " I say.

Laugh if you want.

Call it strange.

Say it's even a little mystical coming out of the mouth of a high school sophomore, let alone one who neither thinks much of herself nor is thought much of by others, who doesn't even comprehend how she memorized it.

But there it is!

The Gandhi quote about mutuality, used as an illustration in Erikson's essay, these words—Mom and Dad!—left my lips at exactly 9:34 A.M. on this, the second meeting with Dr. Rogers during the New Year, in response to his question.

And judging from the ooh's and ah's of people like Tuy, Doty and Tamara and Rosa and Joshua and Tommy to my left and to my right and from my rear, to say nothing of the sparkles in the eyes of the statuesque one poised on the corner of his desk—judging, in short, from a new atmosphere that has settled over the room, I have struck the mother lode.

Pure gold.

Such a feeling!

It is like blasting off from Cape Kennedy, solo, the first and only female in the world to set out on a journey through the Solar System: *Hope Christopherous Gallagher Columbus!*

Tommy, with square jaw, jumps from his seat and says, "The old Golden Rule could coexist with wars as long as wars were limited in scope. But with the advent of atomic bombs, a new rule—based on the ideas of Gandhi and of people like the Adamsons, who trained Elsa, the lioness, an animal, to be loving—a new rule is necessary."

Dr. Rogers propels himself from the desk and rampages up and down the aisles.

"Wonderful! Great! Stupendous! Hurry, someone give the name of the new rule."

Gorgeous Doty, the fringes of her fine hair bouncing at her waist where the scotch plaid skirt begins, screams out, "Mutuality, Dr. Rogers. Erikson refers to the new rule as mutuality: Do nothing that in strengthening you weakens another."

The man, despite his woes, flips.

He grins from ear to ear.

Color surges back into his face.

"Just between countries and nations?" he storms, wild-eyed, lost in an idea.

Joshua, so enraptured he stops stuttering altogether, thrusts his arm up but doesn't even bother to be recognized. "Erikson extends his rule to the relationships between parents and child, between husband and wife, between doctor and patient."

By now, Dr. Rogers is back on the desk's edge. He eyes his shoes.

"Between teacher and student, between"—the mellifluous voice catches—"between teacher . . . and . . . er . . . teacher." His voice topples.

Oh, what a fading away there is now! What a falling off, a dying feebleness to the echo of his words as they sink into a bottomless abyss.

Tuy Nguyen, from the back, his lovely foreign accent juxtaposed (another Rogers contribution to my vocabulary!) with normal American ones, heightens the ecstasy of the moment. This is what education should be all about, mixing things up a little with people from all over the world. Talking up to them, not down at them, as happens in most classrooms. In a near chant, he says, "Like each person in his own life, Dr. Rogers, Erikson says the human race has reached a critical moment in history. Now that there is an atomic bomb, *mankind*"—he stresses the word as if to show Dr. Rogers whose side *he's* on—"*mankind* must mature and become ethical, rather than remain merely moral."

That, too, suddenly comes back to me from the

essay. Until a minute ago, the essay had seemed to me to be nothing more than a ton of pages to be riffled through. Isn't that, after all, the way I've been conditioned to read homework assignments since the beginning? The monotonous voice repeats notes from a lesson plan: "Read from page such-and-such to page so-and-so," and of course, like a puppet, you do.

Dr. Rogers's face lights again.

But the light's not for himself.

It's for us.

"Ladies and gentlemen," he says, "you have made me extremely proud."

How do I know the light's for us?

You can always tell when someone's thinking about you and not themselves from the size and depth of their pupils.

Remember Miss Hotshot during the Christmas holidays in Wardman's Merchandise Center, with all that makeup, who ripped into me? The warning was in her eyes already, except I wasn't bright enough to know it then.

Whatever else might be on Dr. Rogers's mind right this minute, the light in his eyes is for us because we've caught on.

"The whole point of the pilot honors program, ladies and gentlemen, is simply that."

He raises his arm and swings it in an arc across the room.

"If nothing more comes of all this than that, if you can see that the advent of nuclear capabilities has nullified the old Golden Rule and forced us to evolve a new one, if you learn by hard experience to treat one another with respect and esteem instead of hypo- and hypercritically, if you come to understand that we must stop spouting grandiose moralities at one another as we simultaneously cut one another's throats—if you learn these things, the program will have succeeded."

He paces back and forth nervously, searching, digging, plumbing the depths of his brain for more, more.

"If you learn that, and these things, too—that the culture of art and the culture of science must come together, not remain isolated and apart from each other; that science, before this century is over, will be able to, Godlike, manipulate the very basis of life; that the questions are, Do we want to have all that power and will we know what to do with it, and are we prepared to struggle through the reading of more than simpleminded books in order to learn what we must know in order to decide—if the program helps in these ways, that will be more than enough."

I have slunk down in my front row seat, not from weariness, but from the heaviness of a burden.

It will not be easy to be a twenty-first-century leader.

Because in order not to cut someone else's throat, it suddenly occurs to me, you have to learn to respect your own.

Dear God!

Help me to be like the others, not least of all Tuy Nguyen! TIE WIN! TIE WIN!

9

WHAT'S AMAZING is the way every class seems to fit in beautifully with every other one—just about. The program's like a huge mosaic made up of a thousand jagged and ragged pieces, but when you look for them hard and long, why, you can't find the seams.

Joshua is scholarly looking in his glasses when he comes to me a couple of days after Dr. Rogers spoke to us about Erikson. The class has just now finished a discussion of Joseph Conrad's *Heart of Darkness*, and Joshua says, "Um . . . woul . . . would you thin . . . think me push . . . pushy if I call . . . called you Hope?"

Frankly, I'm flattered and honored that he would

want to talk to me at all. He apparently feels as comfortable with me as when he answers a question from Dr. Rogers, his stuttering is so barely noticeable.

"Lord, no, Joshua!" I say.

"C . . . Conrad's story . . . did you find it . . . um . . . harder than . . . er . . . Erikson?"

I nod, but then, much to my amazement, find myself saying, "But do you know what, Joshua? The minute Dr. Rogers talked about Kurtz's crying out, 'The Horror! The Horror!' it hit me."

The torrent pouring from my lips frightens me, that's how unlike the old Hope Gallagher it is. "Kurtz gave in to evil the way each one of us would if the circumstances were right. We're—"

The two of us hyperventilate simultaneously, the significance of what Dr. Rogers pulled out of Tuy Nguyen (TIE WIN! TIE WIN!) and Doty during class rising to the same level of consciousness in each of us at the same time.

"We're all of us pretty much alike, I guess. And that's what ties *Heart of Darkness* in with Erikson." I'm palavering all over the place, one thing's popping into my head so hectically after another.

The goose bumps, of course, have already arrived. But now, in addition, I'm getting something new. In his second class, Dr. Rogers, describing how *ideas*, like sensations, can give you a thrill, referred to T. S. Eliot's concept of "unified sensibility." Only he simplified Eliot's concept by telling us how sometimes, when he himself finally understood an idea he'd been having difficulty understanding, he got *orgiastic chills* up and down his body.

I'm getting one of those now, as I hear myself telling Joshua, "Kurtz had to become immoral in order to . . . if he had lived . . . become ethical, mature, basing his judgments about right and wrong, not on rewards and punishments, but on reason."

Joshua gives me this look.

"Tha . . . that's in . . . incredible, Hope," he says. "*Now* . . . um . . . wha . . . what Dr. Rogers just said fi . . . *finally* makes sense to me."

That very same day we're sitting in Dr. Haggerty's class, and he's meshing major ideas from different disciplines to show us how he'll make history jibe with the other courses.

He is short and frumpy, with barely any hair left and *that* tiny bit helter-skelter over his ears and just above the nape of his neck. He has this uncanny ability to put gestures into dates and names so that the dates and names seem to be prancing before your eyes. The history stops being history and becomes action taking place around you this very moment.

But that isn't all.

As he's going on, he suddenly brings history and science and literature together as if they were one subject.

He says, "Newton—mathematician and physicist—and our Founding Fathers, as unrelated as they seem to be in their interests, share concerns about inertia, don'tcha see? In government, our system of checks and balances, which does so much to make us a distinctive democracy, slows down our ability to make speedy decisions and take impulsive actions."

Oh, how the word "impulsive" strikes home!

"And," he goes on, leaping to the *top* of his desk, "in a state of nature, objects in motion continue in motion unless stopped by an outside force."

He's gesticulating wildly.

He points to the desk top as the force that has stopped him. "What's more," he says, leaping back to the floor now and straightening out his clothing, "what's true of physics and government is equally true of literature. Think of Hamlet's inertia, for instance."

Is this too much or what?

"And . . . and what's true of literature is true of people, us—you, me, the faculty in the program. Inert! Yes, inert!" He scratches his head. "It's easier to stand still, be at zero, than act."

After history, Rosa—whom I'm coming to like immensely, she's so . . . well . . . fragile and delicate but really so strong and decisive at the same time—walks down the hallway with me to Mrs. Courtney's biology lab.

"My parents want me very much to have a fine education, you know, but when I described Dr.

Rogers's new program, they became skeptical. My father said to me, 'Rosa, this does not sound like a traditional curriculum to me. I do not wish to hold you back, but we must give thought to this.' I believe I've liked Dr. Bialek because she is stern, perhaps more than she should be, but that forces you to pay attention in a traditional way."

"I know," I say. "I'm not sure I totally agree that I like her"—I'd like to ask *Rosa* if she knows anything about Bialek and Dr. Rogers, but how can I?—"but on the other hand, the world's certainly big enough for differences of opinion among friends. When I told my folks about the program, they didn't exactly do handstands either."

"But," Rosa says, "I have never understood before how together everything is. Do you know, Hope, what I mean?"

I'm guessing I really do. "It's Dr. Rogers," I say. "To my way of thinking, he's the first authentic teacher I've ever had. And if you take one such brilliant teacher and give him freedom, what results is this terrifically inspiring program."

Then Rosa says something that's so perceptive, it makes me wish I had said it. "Is it not as though all knowledge were one?"

Lord, what an insight!

The mosaic becomes more complete as we take our seats in Mrs. Laura Courtney's biology lab.

She's assigned us tables and partners. I'm teamed with Tamara. Tammy, who has studied my knee holes on more than one occasion since the program started, protects *her* precarious ego by going out of her way to wear extremely *un*revealing clothing. She wears smocks instead of blouses, so that her waist is always invisible.

It is a stroke of fortune that Tammy is my lab partner, for others have told me it's a subject she excels in.

Though she's petite, Mrs. Courtney has this alto voice, which makes it virtually impossible *not* to pay attention to her.

She devotes her opening class to a discussion of advances in molecular biology, specifically to the subject of identifying gene markers on chromosomes.

I will confess that, at the start, I am thinking, *Ho hum!*

Eventually, however, as she begins to allude to the potential for altering genes that carry various diseases, such as bipolar illness or diabetes, I find myself curiously coming out of my stupor.

An article from *Scientific American* she's given us raises the question of whether it's ethical to insert fetal tissue into the brains of adults who suffer from Parkinson's disease.

Doty, *her* waist-long hair frizz free, says, "I think that's really cool, you know? Eliminating life-threatening and disabling diseases."

Tuy, who's been his usual reserved self, suddenly raises his hand.

Mrs. Courtney struggles a bit. "Fire away, Mr. Nguyen?"

"Yes, ma'am," he says. "You have pronounced it correctly." He chooses his words carefully, obviously not wanting to embarrass himself in his second language and also, I think, just generally wishing to keep a low profile. When he smiles, his face—like a bust sculpted out of bronze—exudes energy and confidence. "I would like to comment"—he nods in Doty's direction—"on Ms. McLaughlin's—"

She interrupts him and says, "Please call me Doty, Tuy."

"Yes, Doty," Tuy goes on, "thank you. But I would like to suggest that the idea of genetic manipulation isn't exactly new. And it's somewhat tragic that, in the earlier part of the century, when it was called eugenics, some nations used it as an excuse to annihilate millions of people in order to create a superior human race."

Lord, I'm reacting with the same kinds of chills I'm used to getting only from Dr. Rogers.

Mrs. Courtney, who's obviously impressed, too, says, "Point beautifully taken, Mr. Nguyen. This program has been designed precisely to help us learn where and how and if to draw ethical lines. If we can bring the normally compartmentalized fields of knowledge to bear on one another, with luck we'll not repeat the mistakes of those who created the atomic bomb. Remember, they created it first and then, later, when they saw its effects, some of them committed suicide because they couldn't live with the consequences of their actions."

The room's abuzz with exchanges.

What I couldn't ever have imagined would happen in a million years has.

The intangible camaraderie that seemed to begin at Mooky's has really taken hold.

Like the different disciplines the teachers are trying to unify, we, the students, seem to be becoming of a single mind, too.

But not, I'm sorry to say, in the last class of the day, Dr. Bialek's, which she told us earlier in the week would deal with philosophy.

Bad tastes, I suppose, linger in most everyone's mouth after what she did on Monday at the orientation—despite Rosa's efforts to help us understand.

In fact, *I* become Bialek's target number two the minute we all settle in at 2:00 P.M.

I sit in *her* last row.

As I take my seat, she says to me, "There's nothing wrong with jeans, young lady, but you owe it to the other women of the world to present yourself neatly."

I try to gulp down the knot that's raced into my throat, dazed and humiliated by the unexpected onslaught. What in God's name is going on with her? If she's in the program voluntarily, why's she going out of her way trying to destroy everything? Has she lost her beans or something?

"I don't know why you can't sew or patch them. Women have enough to contend with without having to worry about those who feed into male chauvinism by dressing provocatively."

Let me be patient and tolerant, Lord, please!

Talk about making sexist statements! This woman's really stressed out for some reason.

Rosa—God bless her!—rushes in with "Ahem, Dr. Bialek. May I ask you if we will have a reading list for philosophy as we did in your class last semester?"

Bialek veers sharply off course, away from me—as though I were an ant she's flicked off her picnic plate—to Rosa.

"Yes, Rosa," she says. "Of course we will."

Her sheared-off granite voice turns to sand; the beady, predatory eyes suddenly soften to opal.

From thoughts of suicide, my brain leaps to murder.

Visions of Dr. Rogers, paralyzed during the orientation seminar by her . . . her . . . crassness? madness? . . . flash before my eyes.

I sink into oblivion in my chair.

Bialek proceeds, after Rosa's interruption, as though nothing has happened:

"The intellectual currents of the three centuries I will focus on in this program all come together in our own century to culminate, not in the *ascent* of humans but in their *descent*, as was so well depicted by Bronowski, in his series on ma—that is to say, in his wonderful series tracing the sociological and philosophical evolution of peoples."

Tammy makes the mistake of whispering to another member of the group, Pamela Chomolieski, "Isn't that ironic? Speaking of descent *here?*"

"I *beg* your pardon," Bialek cries out, stony voiced again.

Tammy turns gray.

"Would you mind repeating what you just said?"

The veins on Bialek's hand wriggle like worms in the mud as she grips the lectern where she's standing.

In a sliver of a response, Tammy ekes out, "I didn't mean anything, ma'am. Sometimes my mouth moves faster than my brain."

"We'll see about that," she bellows. "I don't know who recommended you, but we'll certainly see about that."

When she dismisses class, we flee as from a wake.

If not for my deep reverence for him, I would not *want* to understand how and why Dr. Rogers picked this . . . this person . . . for his team. But a person's got to speculate now—in every direction.

10

DURING the next several weeks, the Bialek thing *really* gets out of hand.

One day, for instance, she's just finished lecturing on eighteenth-century rationalism and nature.

Tuy—as his hand shoots up to be recognized, it flashes in on me that I *dreamed* about him last night!—breathlessly says, "I am not positive I comprehend *why* the rationalists put such complete faith in the preeminence of reason over emotion."

Bialek doesn't waste a second.

"Shut up!" she screams.

Wait a minute!

He's made a perfectly innocent and highly intelligent comment, for God's sake!

His native language isn't even English!

If my life depended on it, I wouldn't have known enough even to think what Tuy has said.

Out of the corner of my eye, I see a tear gathering momentum on Doty's eyelid.

Lord Almighty! What in heaven's name's wrong with this woman?

Doty blurts out, "Dr. Rogers would never talk to us—"

Hell breaks loose!

"Don't you tell me about Dr. Rogers, *do you hear me*? He's ruined enough lives."

Doty shrinks.

A stillness falls over the room that's so heavy you want to choke.

But who in God's name would dare?

"You *will* reread the chapter I assigned, Mr. Nguyen. You *will* find a thorough discussion of this issue in that chapter."

Then she tosses this icy-eyed stare at Doty.

"In *my* class that man's name's taboo, do you hear me?"

Another time, we've had to read a long excerpt from Rousseau's *Emile*, which is about the *ideal* way to educate children.

Joshua asks, "Um . . . Dr. . . . Dr. Bial . . . Bialek, ma'am?"

"*Dr.* Bialek is just fine. You don't need to refer to me as ma'am."

By now, of course, Joshua's absolutely in a dither. "I . . . er . . . ah . . ."

Lord, I'm praying, *give Joshua the strength to show her a thing or two.*

It's a commentary on his inner resources that, despite Bialek's attitude, he starts over again, this time, if anything, with greater determination.

"What I . . . I wanted to ask was isn't it sort of . . ."

I've got my fingers crossed that he just keeps going like this, nonstop, to show her and some other people what it means to have courage.

"Isn't it . . . er . . . a paradox that a person who abandoned his own children to a foundling hospital should have written an important work about . . . educating . . . educating . . . er . . . other . . . other people's . . . uh . . . children?"

Bless you, Joshua Melamed!

Thank you!

Keep you!

You did it!

Later, as though Bialek's aiming right for her heart and trying to destroy her, she calls on Doty.

"Define 'perfectibility' as eighteenth-century thinkers used it."

A tear reappears on Doty's eyelid, frozen in dread this time. In an eagerness to please, she replies, "Eighteenth-century thinkers believed that in a state of nature man was basically good."

Bialek explodes. "That's *irrelevant*! I didn't ask about states of nature—I asked about 'perfectibility.'"

After class, her one tear having thawed and begun to proliferate, Doty sobs, "That's it, Hope. I've had it. I think we all gotta talk about this woman."

Rosa's right behind us. She becomes defensive, but if you study her closely, you realize that even *she*'s having a hard time.

"I believe," Rosa says, "she is doing more graduate work, in addition to planning very carefully for this program. It may be, she is overworked, distraught over—"

Doty rushes in. "Man, oh, man, but I never knew a woman could . . ."

Her hair's swishing back and forth along her waistline.

Joshua and Tammy and Tommy join us.

"Let's have lunch at Mooky's," Tommy says.

From out of nowhere, Tuy's suddenly in our midst.

"May I," he says, "go with all of you, too?"

All of a sudden, my dream of him returns.

Which means I've got to get to Heather immediately.

It's not just Bialek's deterioration I have to inform her about.

Now it's the cotillion, too. She's got to know I'm thinking that the whole family's going to have to get used to the idea of my asking someone from Asia to take me.

At the end of fifth period, we all traipse over to Mooky's and fight our way through to our favorite booth at the far end.

We get condescending stares from some of our compatriots.

But so it goes.

A few morons—the ones who get turned on by knocking others—yell out things like "Whoa! Watch out now! Here come the *brains*!" or "C'mon now, poopsy babies! Ain't ya gonna smile?"

Rosa and Tammy turn red as beets.

Doty turns, period.

I'm quaking in my shoes. By exerting tremendous effort, I manage with a smirk not to give them the satisfaction of knowing just how susceptible to their leers I am. I stuff myself into the deepest recess of the booth.

Out of sight, as they say, out of mind.

Joshua takes charge of the orders. Tommy helps him bring the two huge trays of burgers, fries, and Cokes to the table.

Tuy starts things off.

"If," he says, "we do not do something to—how do you say?—transform the way this woman treats us, I am fearful."

For reasons too deep for me, I can't stop staring at him!

It's probably irreverent, inasmuch as we have this mutinous mission, but I'm thinking, *What in God's name's happening to me?*

Rosa appears to be casually and innocently nibbling at her burger, but clearly she's troubled.

She's squinting, deep furrows creasing her forehead.

Tuy goes on, barely touching his burger. "I don't think that woman," he says, "has respect for the dignity of human beings."

His teeth are clenched, and his skin has taken on a purple coloration.

"It's—how shall I say it?—not proper for a teacher to humiliate students in front of their peers."

What care he takes with language!

He's gaining momentum, forgetting his shyness. "We are not children," he says. "Dr. Rogers has established a philosophical, almost a religious basis for our program."

His "philosophical" and "religious" practically make me flip, they're so exactly the words that've echoed inside me since the opening session.

More and more, he sounds like Dr. Rogers, his words seeming separate things from him, for which he, like Dr. Rogers, serves as a medium, a means of transport to the world at large.

Tommy says, "I agree, Tuy. But what're we gonna do?"

Doty puts into words what yours truly, at least,

has begun to wonder. "Maybe the two of them are lovers and they've had a fight?"

I tell you right off, hearing it come out of someone else's mouth hurts a lot more than I expected.

"Doty," I rush in, whether I believe what I'm saying is irreverent or not, "you're being gross."

She shrugs, then digs into her hamburger.

Rosa lays her hamburger down.

"Please don't think of me as a spoilsport," she says, "for I, too, agree that Dr. Bialek's behavior has been bad." She sighs. "But Doty, though her yelling at you is inexcusable, you really shouldn't jeopardize another person's reputation. It is true that for some reason Dr. Bialek is completely different from the way she was. But isn't the right thing to do to go to her and ask her directly why? Tell her what effect she is having?"

What *I'm* thinking is that the right thing is for me to talk to Heather. Immediately!

"Ahem," I interject. "Rosa's right. Instead of making idle accusations, why don't we talk at least to Dr. Rogers?"

Tuy says, "I do believe, Hope Gallagher, you ought to represent us."

The blood rushes to my face.

Tammy and Joshua and Doty and Tommy, in unison, say, "Right on, Hope. You be our emissary."

It's an awkward charge they've laid on me, but how can I tell them why?

I'm not sure I know myself.

"Okay," I say. "I'll try to make an appointment as soon as possible."

I sound a lot more glib about it than I feel.

It isn't even the twenty-first century yet, and they've already thrust me into a leadership role.

Lord, oh, Lord! I'm not ready for this! I'm just a high school sophomore, for God's sake! I can hardly take care of myself, let alone others.

What if I botch it?

What if I let them all down?

"I . . . er . . . uh," I stumble. "Sure you don't want Tuy or Doty or one of you others to—"

With a single voice, they scream out, "You're the one, Hope. C'mon."

Despite all my inadequacies, I reluctantly nod.

Some forks in the road, well . . . people don't let you run from them, no matter how much you'd like to.

There's so much now I've got to tell Heather about.

11

THAT NIGHT, after dishes, I catch her in her room reading something called *The Sweet Rush of Passion*.

"We've got to talk, okay?" I say, shutting the door behind me.

She lays her book down beside her on the bed.

Whether because of our Christmas exchange or not, I don't know, but somehow, now as I look at her, I'm struck by the fact that she's mature for someone who's been out of high school only a short time.

Maybe I'm comparing her in my mind's eye to idiotic-looking me or even to people like

Rosa—whom I truly think highly of—and Doty and Tammy.

I don't know.

But it's not as though *they*'re not mature and brilliant.

It's that she looks more like an *adult*.

"What's up?" she says.

My head feels like a witch's caldron. Do I begin with these alien sensations Tuy's evoked? Or related emotions elicited by Dr. Rogers? Or, maybe worse than anything, what's turning out to be intense, irrational jealousy over Cynthia Bialek, who's done only *one* thing wrong to me during my entire life but whom I already despise as though she'd spent a lifetime torturing me? And what . . . what about . . . yes, what about the mission I've been assigned by the group to accomplish? Oh, sure. It's flattering to know they'd come to *me* during a time of crisis. But where, dear Lord, do I get the guts to walk into Dr. Rogers's office and ask what I'm supposed to ask or say what I'm supposed to say?

"Heather," I plunge on, "if ever anybody needed advice, I do."

I sink down beside her on the bed, covering my knee holes.

She's so neat looking it embarrasses me.

Now I can see why Dad sometimes does a double take when he compares *my* jeans to *Heather's* usual attire.

"Well," she says, "if I can give some, I will."

Then she laughs, so that her dimples pop out on her cheeks.

I wonder, *Does part of her beauty come from the inside out? Is that maybe what makes Dr. Rogers the person he is and Tuy Nguyen who he is, too?*

How to start?

Instead of asking her again what she meant that first time she connected Bialek and Dr. Rogers, I set right in to telling her about the first seminar and Bialek's rude and crude interruption of Dr. Rogers's lecture.

She barges in before I can finish.

"Wow! I didn't think it would ever come to that!"

I grab both her wrists and shake her.

"C'mon, Heather, don't fool around this time," I scream. "I've got to know. I just have to."

She tosses her hair off to the right, presses her lips tightly together, clenches her teeth as though she's got this great conflict going on inside and doesn't know whether to let it all hang out or not.

"Um," she begins, "it's not right to fool with people's reputations, Hope. You know that."

"Don't!" I tell her. "Just help me understand."

She clasps her hands on her lap and stares off at the Matisse print that hangs over her desk.

"That night . . . that night," she says, "when you came home and talked about the honors program Dr. Rogers had started, I have to tell you the news jolted me. I nearly forgot myself and started jabbering right then."

"What nobody understands," I say, "is why he would've asked her to be on the team when—"

Heather stares at me in wonder.

"My God, Hope!" she whispers. Now her eyes dart to the door, on the lookout for Mom or Dad. "Nearly everyone at Livingston knew. Nearly everyone knew—a semester, two, after Rogers arrived—that, married or not, something . . ."

What's the point in her finishing?

Life's lost its meaning!

The knot in my throat turns to mush. I'm going to drown in my own grief!

Heather takes my hand.

"Right after he came," she says, "people said, 'Oh, he's so charismatic, so great, d'ya know? Take his class if you can.' I wanted to, too, except that a friend of mine—do you remember Leslie Gordon?—who had him in English that first—or was it the second?—semester tells me one day—"

Heather stops and drops her head.

"One day, Leslie tells me at lunch, 'I wonder about this guy, you know? Every time he interprets a story, it seems the story's got some sexual meaning.' Well, you know Leslie Gordon. She's slightly melodramatic, so, of course, I didn't pay too much attention. But then I start hearing the same stuff from some other kids. And . . . well . . . maybe I'm a dummy or something, but I just decided I'd skip him."

She breaks off again.

Already my mind's racing backward in time to his classes. Oh, sure, sure. He *did* talk about the use of phallic symbols, I remember, in Steinbeck's "The Chrysanthemums." I remember that! And . . . and . . . then there was Joyce Carol Oates's story "In the Region of Ice," where he said *the nun*, for God's sake, was having second thoughts about her sexuality the minute that mentally ill student entered her college Shakespeare course. And . . . and Williams's "The Use of Force," which we all thought was just about a plain old doctor checking a kid's throat to see if she had diphtheria, but Dr. Rogers comes along and points out the bleeding mouth and the tongue depressor and the doctor's saying he's already fallen in love with the savage brat. Could it be that . . . ?

No! That's just not a lech's look in his eyes! No way!

"Well, Heather," I'm insisting now, "Dr. Rogers *is* charismatic! And . . . and I don't see what's wrong with his interpretations of stories, either."

She throws me a sidelong glance.

"Hope," she says, "don't you see? Sure, I'm not denying he's charismatic. In fact, if anything, I'm agreeing with you. And that's where Cynthia Bialek comes in."

Now she's got me really confused.

"What . . . what're you talking about?" I say, as

though Cynthia Bialek's the farthest thing from my mind right now.

Heather sighs.

"The semester I graduated, the two of them team-taught an English-philosophy course. For God's sake, you never saw one but the other was right next door. It was *the* rumor of the semester, how the two of them were so cozy-cozy."

Things suddenly begin to fall into place. Into horrible, ugly, despicable place.

"But when she interrupted him that first orientation session and ranted about sexism—" I whimper.

"I'd give you a week's salary, Hope, that Bialek fell for the man, and he, being married and having a family—whether he led her on, on purpose or accidentally, really doesn't make a difference—he did this typically sexist thing—you even said that was the word she used when she interrupted him!—and told her to just take a walk when it was too late for her to quit the program. Or maybe he didn't, either—what difference does it make when?—but instead told her, 'You've misunderstood what you call my charisma' . . . and . . . and the rest is history. Hell just hath no fury like a woman scorned!"

"Are . . . are you . . . ? Heather, you swear? On the Bible?"

She furrows her forehead and squints at me.

That's her answer?

I don't know how I'm supposed to face Dr. Rogers now with complaints about Bialek.

If Heather's even halfway right, he—Dr. Everett Rogers—ought to be the one to go.

That's not what I say, though.

Because it's not all that clear in my head what's right, what's wrong.

"The honors group nominated me to go to Dr. Rogers and talk to him about Bialek and the mess she's causing."

Heather grabs her hair and falls backward full out on her bed.

"You're kidding me," she says.

"I am *not*," I tell her.

"God," she says, "I'm glad I'm not in your shoes."

I've never felt so addled in my life. Everything's coming to this gigantic head that could explode any second. You put your faith and trust in somebody for the first time in your life; then this whole bunch of people come around poking holes into him, as if he were already hanging in effigy. And, frankly speaking, I don't like it.

I don't like it at all.

People make mistakes!

What's the big deal about that?

If everybody's so blasted perfect they can afford to be hypercritical of others, well, then, let them be.

Still and all, *he* goes ahead and talks about mutuality and the Golden Rule and seems to be practicing it, but brother, first chance *he* gets . . . Brother! What about *her*?

I turn to leave.

"Thanks for the advice, Heather. That really helped!"

It's not until after I get to my bedroom and bury my head under the pillow that I remember that I forgot to tell her about Tuy and the Spring Cotillion.

But if you can't even trust the people you . . . you . . . well, why even *think* of rose gardens like Sophomore Spring Cotillion?

12

WEIRDER and weirder occurrences cast additional shadows on the program the whole next week.

The thing's got me so unnerved, I'm walking around in a kind of stupor from one place to another, fingering my split ends as if there's no tomorrow.

So that when, for instance, Mr. Foster Johnson, my freshman-year art teacher, sneaks up behind me one day between classes and nearly gives me a heart attack by remarking "I don't suppose you talk to normal teachers anymore, do you, Hope Gallagher?"—when he does that, my emotions go all haywire, for God's sake!

Here, all through freshman art—which is a course I chose on my own, thinking maybe I'd find my niche in life in that particular area of endeavor—that whole first year Mr. Johnson said about this much to me.

Now, a year later—when I wouldn't have thought he'd remember me from Eve—Mr. Johnson comes up on me from nowhere as if I'd been his pet.

Is he sniping at the honors program or alluding to Dr. Rogers and Bialek?

When I mention the incident to Rosa, she tells me, "It's strange, Hope, but some of my former teachers are treating me, too, with—what shall I call it?—greater detachment. It's as if, by being a member of Dr. Rogers's honors program, we have estranged ourselves from members of the faculty who are not."

And then, the next day, Tammy tells me, "Would you believe, Hope, what they told me in the counseling office when I went in this morning to inquire about whether it was the PSAT or the SAT that determined whether a person qualified as a National Merit finalist?"

"What?" I ask.

"The secretary snickered and said, 'Oh, you're in the special honors program, dearie, aren't you? Where some of the teachers are so *earthy*, I'm shocked you'd even bother to ask.' I nearly fell over, Hope." Then Tammy pauses, looks suspiciously around us, and whispers, "I think we'd better get used to it. I think some of the older faculty here're gettin' crazy over a *kid* like Dr. Rogers receiving so much administrative attention."

Is it, I'm thinking, *"administrative attention" or lascivious sneers, damn it?*

Tammy's got mental telepathy or something, that's for certain, because, when I enter the gym first period, who should be waiting just for me but "older faculty" member Ms. Slender Perfecto Philbon. She's wearing the gold-stripe spandex pants, her silver stopwatch dangling from a chain around her neck right into her declivity.

"Well, now, Gallagher," she says in a very throaty voice, "you truly surprise me."

To say I'm taken aback by her tone of voice and choice of words is an understatement of the first order.

Picture the scene:

My brain's abuzz with a trillion and one complications, practically each one dealing with the meaning of life.

The furthest thought from my mind is physical education and Olympic-style medalists with perfect bodies.

I've blundered my way from the locker room into the gym by some form of unthinking, reflex behavior.

The last, but the very *last* human being in the world I wish to exchange words with at this moment is this woman, particularly when the words are a cryptic "You truly surprise me." I haven't the foggiest notion what she's referring to, since it's clear I haven't lost any weight since the last time we saw each other and I can't think of what else she'd want from me.

"Beg . . . er . . . I beg your pardon, Ms. Philbon?" I respond, my voice rising somewhat in consternation. After all, for nearly two years now—when I've come to gym at all—the only words she's had with me have in some way been related to commands to run or jump or bend or sit—that's all. *"You truly surprise me!"* For *what?* I'm wondering.

I give myself a superquick going-over to see if, absentmindedly, I've left an article of clothing off or, more likely, split my gym suit along some seam or other.

"Don't think," she says, pulling me off to the side where the mats are stacked against the wall, "don't think I'm unaware of the number of times you've cut gym, Gallagher."

My heart sinks.

Here it comes finally!

At last, she's going to let me have it!

"Yes'm," I mutter, staring holes into the gym floor in total terror.

The gang may have nominated me to represent them in a meeting with Dr. Rogers. But I haven't by any stretch of the imagination developed the assertiveness yet to deal in anything above a whisper with Ms. Philbon.

"If you think your being in this newfangled, immoral honors program of what's his name is going to exempt you from normal Livingston requirements . . . well, young lady . . . let me tell you, you've got another think coming, d'ya understand me?"

If you've ever been a maggot at the bottom of a garbage can, you might be able to guess at how I'm squirming around now.

Because if I "yes'm" again, it's not me getting hurt that's important. It's Dr. Rogers. And whatever he's done . . . if he's done anything or not . . . it's just not right, not having a chance to face your accuser, especially when my cutting gym's never, never had anything to do with him, so what's she making false accusations for?

A thunderhead—a monstrosity of a storm cloud—sucks me up into its dead center, and these flashes of lightning are banging around inside me until I can't stand it anymore.

Whatever ambivalences toward Dr. Rogers have begun to mushroom inside me, he doesn't deserve flogging from Philbon. No way!

"I know I've been derelict in the past, ma'am," I say, "but . . ." Something new, a feeling I've never experienced before, surges up inside me, making my skin tingle as if I were—dear God!—molting or something and I'm crawling out of my very own self into a new me, into, into a *person*, believe it or not, that someone's just gone ahead and stepped on, and let me tell you, it does *not*, I repeat *not*, feel very good. And if it doesn't feel good to me, it sure won't feel good to him either if *he* ever finds out how loosely she's tossing allegations around. So . . . so . . . somehow or other I've got to, just have to say something. Otherwise—Lord!—how'm I gonna know who I really am, what I really believe about people? And if you don't know that, what's . . . what's the point of going on living? "But, Ms. Philbon, if you'll excuse me, ma'am, Dr. Rogers's honors program . . ." If I'm bumbling around, it's because speaking out, saying what I really think . . . well . . . it's all still absolutely new to me, even though I'm fifteen years old already, for God's sake! "His program, ma'am"—I grope for words—"his program's not the cause of my cutting . . ." I'm praying hard for courage. Dear Lord! Let me be understanding and patient. Let me not judge when I'm so imperfect myself. "Of my cutting physical education classes." It's beginning to feel to me like peeling off the layers of a rotten onion, the reek getting stronger with each peel. "He's got nothing to do with . . . with . . ."

Oh, God, it's so difficult to face reality! To look it in the eye and say, "Damn it! I'm not running away from you anymore. What's true is true, and you can't let someone else take the blame for it!"

"Dr. Rogers's wonderful new program's got absolutely nothing to do with my cuts." My colon's more spastic than it's ever been. What if, what if he led Bialek— No, it's too hard to believe! But, on the other hand, there's no hiding anymore, either. "I've cut . . . I've cut . . . because of . . . because of . . . my obesity, that's what, which, if you want to know the truth, ma'am, is the only, I mean the only cause of my cutting gym, the humiliation of it, not Dr. Rogers."

Oh, wow!

I got it out!

It can't be retrieved.

I feel faint.

Woozy all over.

But if all hell's going to break loose, let it!

I've got a little scorn and fury, too!

It's too late for games now!

She can't be allowed to blame a maybe innocent man for *my* problems because, because he's not only *not* to blame for them, he's the only person alive who's ever consciously—whatever is going on between him and that, that . . . witch—ever consciously tried to make me believe in myself.

Ms. Gold-Striped Spandex stands there, stunned.

Her mouth's hanging open.

The blood's rushed to her cheeks.

Her silver stopwatch's actually quivering in the declivity!

She hems a little.

She haws a little.

She turns this way and then that way, looking for an escape.

Finally, she finds some words. My mouth falls open when I see her lips forming my name. "Hope, can you accept an apology?"

Sure I can, Ms. Philbon. Try me.

She laughs, faintly.

"We teachers, I think, really do fit that old adage, you know?"

I shake my head. No, I don't know which adage she's talking about.

"You know: Those who can, do; those who can't, teach." She fiddles with her stopwatch. "Or preach." When she looks up, I get a peek at her pupils, and darn it all to heck if they don't seem sincerely remorseful. "I guess we're such passive creatures, we sometimes fill our lives with and thrive on jealousies and rivalries and rumors." She eyes the students massing in the center of the gym. "What I said to you was crude and stupid and hurtful." Then she just about wipes me out by taking my arm. "What you said about obesity and humiliation—that, Hope, took courage. I'm genuinely sorry I jumped to such a farfetched conclusion."

It's not everything, but it'll do.

"Thanks, Ms. Philbon," I say. "I don't think anyone's ever called me courageous before."

13

LATER THAT DAY, when I see Tuy, I'm—forgive the pun!—more hopeful than I've been lately. And resolute.

"Two things," I say.

My heart's pounding.

"Why, yes, Hope," he says, genteelly enough for me to want to cry. "Of course."

"First is, I'm going to see if I can get in to talk to Dr. Rogers now."

A penetrating smile spreading across his lips ignites sparks throughout my body.

"That is why, Hope," he says, "the group selected you. You are a woman of action. And compassion, too."

God save me! He's bathed me with so much of his warmth, I'm embarrassed to look into his eyes.

"Second," I stammer, "second is . . . er . . ."

Woman of action, indeed! If only he knew the excruciating pain rampaging through me now as I prepare to take the initiative, turning centuries of Gallagher etiquette topsy-turvy to ask him to the cotillion. Lord, it's scary! What if, for instance, he says, "Go suck on a lemon, Hope Gallagher. I'm going with someone else." Or . . . or "Sorry, old girl! I don't respond favorably to invitations proffered to me by females." Or worse than either, "Where I come from, kiddo, any woman who'd initiate this kind of discussion with a man is, shall I say, a shameful hussy, a disgrace to her gender, a blight and scourge to *ideal womanhood*!"

What if?

On the other hand, the twenty-first century's not all that far off, either.

I shoot a glance at him. Oh, his hair! It's all smoothed back, but not in any kind of putrid way that you know is intentional.

The good old goose bumps begin, the same variety as those that normally come out only for you know who!

"Is it just me?" I say. "Or is it really hot today?"

We're standing in the Levian Wing, just around the corner from Room 272, Dr. Rogers's office.

He says, "I do believe you're correct, Hope."

Lord! Lord! Lord! Don't let me make a fool of either of us!

"Er . . . uh . . . did you . . . oh . . . ever"—I take the plunge—"did you ever hear of the Livingston Sophomore Spring Cotillion?"

He leans toward me as though he hasn't caught what I've said—would I kindly repeat it?

"The Sophomore Cotillion?"

His face reddens.

"Perhaps you will think me foolish, Hope," he says. "But though I do believe I know what a cotillion is, no, I cannot say I have heard of the Livingston Sophomore Cotillion."

There's a kind of innocence about him that makes you just want to reach over and take his hand and explain everything about why girls make such a big deal over it.

I can't quite bring myself to do that yet, but I explain.

He nods.

But so far, that's all!

I can't tell for sure whether he's getting my hint or not.

The good old knot in my throat's starting to stick. *Good God, Gallagher!* I tell myself. *If you want to play it safe, why not go live in a test tube?*

"The reason I bring the matter up, Tuy," I blurt out as fast as it'll come, "the reason is . . . um . . . uh . . . I wonder . . . would you like to accompany me to the cotillion?"

There!

It's out!

There's no taking it back now.

Tuy suddenly gives me those eyes of his as he never has before.

"I am extremely flattered that you have chosen to ask me, Hope," he says. "And . . . and of course my answer is yes. But will it not displease you to know that I cannot dance?"

Oh, Lord!

Is that all?

"Neither can I," I rush to point out, knowing full well what it's like being out there alone. "But . . . but so far as I know, that's not a requirement for going."

He laughs.

We glance at each other in what you might call a fleeting manner.

"This excellent invitation of yours, Hope, certainly puts the problems at school in a new light."

The problems at school?

In a new light!

God, I'd forgotten—*in the light of new insight.*

What an appropriate allusion to Erikson's essay!

He and Dr. Rogers are so much alike, it's frightening!

But that's not all either, it suddenly dawns on me.

There's Kurtz, too, dear Lord!

That "horror" Joshua and I talked about.

Each and every one of us—not just Kurtz, but

Dr. Rogers, Bialek, me, Tuy—has it inside us to do the unexpected under the right circumstances, whether good or bad!

Shoot!

Nothing's clear-cut.

I pull back a foot.

"Well," I say. "It's that critical moment for me." Tuy cannot possibly know how our brief conversation has strengthened me. I take a deep, deep breath. "I'm going to go in and see Dr. Rogers now. Maybe they can talk, he can get her to . . . to . . . behave in class . . . at least, and . . . uh . . . she can get revenge later."

Tuy stares quizzically at me but doesn't pick up on the tryst allusion. Instead, he walks beside me to Dr. Rogers's office and becomes the second person in a day to say, "You are truly courageous, Hope."

It's *really* true! Good and bad junk comes in bunches.

That might go a good distance helping me do what I have to do next.

From a position just outside Room 272, I watch Tuy vanish down the corridor.

My palms turn clammy in my isolation.

I shut my eyes for a moment and dream: *How will it be when Tuy comes to the house to meet everybody?*

God, but I hope they like him!

14

IT'S MY FIRST private meeting with Dr. Rogers since the invitation before Christmas.

I'm shaky when I enter.

This is not the same man who said to me, "Beautiful paper, young lady. Top-notch job of thinking."

No way!

The more conservative clothing's not precisely the difference. Given the humiliation at Bialek's hands, that might be expected. But . . . well . . . the aura's gone. Totally!

Take his eyes, for instance. The gleam's missing.

Maybe, I'm thinking, *he's hiding the guilt of clandestine relationships.*

Maybe his wife's confronted him about his cha-
risma.

Who knows?

He turns to me where I'm straddling the threshold of the doorway and clearing my throat with an "ahem!"

A ghastly pallor covers his face.

A book lies open in his hands, which rest against the edge of his desk. I think, *He's deep in thought—don't disturb him.*

"Hello, Ms. Gallagher," he says.

The music's vanished from his voice.

I don't know whether to stay or leave.

He doesn't need *me* in the middle of his life. If everything Heather's told me is true, he's got enough to worry about.

But then he says, "What can I do for you?" forcing a smile.

Barely emboldened, I inch across the threshold, still avoiding his eminently sad eyes.

Despite myself, the twitch that twitched the first time I saw and heard him twitches still!

And now, too, I become self-conscious about my jeans.

I'm not sure why.

They feel out of place for some reason.

"I don't know how . . ." I stumble, fumble, grope, fail. "What I mean is . . ."

It's hell when you know what you'd like to say

but can't because it's foreign territory and you could end up going off the deep end, even though your heart says, *Go do it, for heaven's sake, before the ship sinks and takes you and him and maybe everybody else down, too.*

Silence drowns out the tiny noises that usually fill his office.

"Tuy Nguyen . . ." I start. But then it occurs to me, *No, moron! Don't mention names!* "The group . . . er . . ." Since *she*, Dr. Bialek, hasn't yet told *me* to "shut up" or labeled anything I've said (which in her class is nothing) as "irrelevant" but merely objected to my jeans, I feel awkward. I'm not directly involved. So why bother? On the other hand, I've been nominated to plead the cause of others. *Don't haggle over trivia,* I remind myself. "The honors group, sir, it's . . . well . . . um . . . there's a mutiny brewing over the way Dr. Bialek's been treating . . . Well, the others asked me . . ."

Dr. Rogers shifts in his chair.

"Oh," he says, his voice flat. He crosses his arms and eyes the beige bookcase. "I shouldn't have waited for you to . . ."

Whatever ugly feelings I've had evaporate. The man's in despair!

"You don't have to—" I say.

"Yes, I do," he mumbles. "I owe it to *you*, at least. And the others. You could have said no when I asked you to . . ."

He shrugs. He shakes his head.

I can't believe I'm doing this.

This is high school!

I'm a sophomore!

Why'm I here?

"I heard," he says. "I knew." He hangs his head. *He*'s got a pressure building in him, too. But he's got to go on. "I heard from other sources that she'd started acting out, but"—he struggles even to say the words—"but things paralyzed me."

His face is covered with shame or guilt, I can't guess which. He rubs the furrows of his brow. *Acting out what?* I'm thinking. *Who else has talked to him?*

"Er . . ." I say. "Actually . . . uh . . . you see, Dr. Rogers . . ."

Regardless of what Heather's told me about him, whether someone else has gotten to him first about Bialek or not, the simple fact remains that right now my bones ache for the man.

"Yes . . . er . . . actually, sir, that's why I came . . . um . . . to see you."

He grimaces.

He signals me to go on.

"Tuy Nguyen, Joshua Melamed, Doreen McLaughlin . . . the others, sir . . . we . . . you see . . . we're supposed to be honors students, right?" I breathe deeply. "So it isn't justice to . . ." The line from Gandhi haunts me. "It's not fair for her to harm us just because she's the teacher. . . ." Now *I'm* ashamed to look at him. "Yessir. She's told several students to shut up or accused them of saying irrelevant things. *You* never do. . . ."

It's hard to believe that I, who have slogged my way through all my schooling, am here with him in the name of dignity in education.

And tattling, no less.

Tattling on a teacher in *his* program, with whom he's possibly . . . No, it's impossible; he couldn't . . .

"Several students have met and want to—"

"Mr. Sloan's told me," Dr. Rogers says. "I should have acted bef—" He stops short, stares at the still-open book resting against the edge of the desk. His jaw's set hard and square, but the funny thing is, despite that, he looks soft, malleable. He speaks to the air. "I didn't act before—when I should have. Inertia caused by the recognition of my own insensitivities . . . the hurts I . . ."

Are all the rumors true, then?

Something in him is changing. Right before my eyes. Nameless, invisible, impalpable, like a drop in barometric pressure.

My heart's thumping. My knees are up against his desk.

He laughs a self-disapproving laugh.

"And *I* tried to teach all of *you* about those crises in life that test us. About the self-righteous Kurtzes of the world who show us what we're capable . . ." He's talking to some far-off target, past the office, past the school building.

"I'm sorry, sir," I mumble. "I don't . . ."

He sets the book down on his desk, interlacing his fingers and squeezing them until they turn white at the knuckles. He rises, takes a step or two.

The office feels tight, small, like a prison. Like a desperate animal, he starts to pace, around the desk, up against his bookcase, fingering a book here, a pile of papers there, the features of his face slipping and sliding so that there's no way to know *what's* inside.

Then suddenly he stops, clutches the back of his chair, and seems, for the *first* time seems to understand that we're in the office together. "I owe it to *you* . . . to explain . . . what's been . . ."

Oh, the twitching!

He's fingering his long hair, as if the answer or the message or whatever he's hunting for were there somewhere, and so he's got to get at it, no matter what the cost.

"The baby, you see . . ."

He doesn't know I'm there anymore. An emptiness is at the center of his eyes and, though he's facing me, he's staring right through me. "It didn't seem right, not to do something to keep her memory alive."

My knees crush up against the hard desk; arrows of pain pierce every part of my body. Oh, my God! *His baby?*

I can't say how.

I can't say why.

But what my gut's telling me is that it's as though

we're in a confessional, only he's doing the confessing and I'm doing the listening, not because he wants it to be that way, but because, dear Lord, he can't help it—this incredible pain's surging up inside him, overwhelming his better judgment.

He looks at me now as through a mist, squinting.

I fight to hold the tears back. I've got to be strong for him, no matter what's happened.

But he shakes his head.

"It's okay to cry, Ms. Gallagher," he says. "I did. My wife did." He gives me his handkerchief. Our hands nearly touch. "But then, you know, I thought, well . . . one has to make it mean something, do you see?"

I nod, except that I don't know what in God's name I see or don't see.

"So I said to my wife," he says, "I said, 'Let's keep her memory alive in some positive way.' And the day we buried her"—he walks away, his back toward me, his voice rising—"that day, it came to me." He stops abruptly, laughs in an eerie way. "My wife didn't even know what I was—" He spins on his heels, facing me, the laugh fading into this self-loathing mutter. "I'd already been thinking about the program anyway, talked it over with Dr. Bia—" He pulls up short, his face beet red. "The people here were so wonderful, so supportive at first."

I'm churning in places I never knew I had, gripping the edge of the desk, hanging on for dear life.

He changes course.

"It came to me to—you understand?—memorialize Christie in an exciting, innovative, different approach to students, to education . . . aiming *up* at their intellects, not *down* at that mediocrity that squirms in everyone if we let it. But after the others . . . Dr. Bialek . . . committed themselves to it . . ." He finds a bare spot on top of the bookcase, sets his elbows on it, his head drooping into his knuckles. "But I couldn't live with my own duplicity. . . . I had to break off. . . . For everyone's sake, I had to. . . ."

I want to tell him, "If not for that computer glitch, I'd never have been put in your English honors class, and if I'd never been put in your English honors class, I'd probably never have met you. . . . Well, anyway, you'd never have invited me to join the program, and I'd never be hearing, hearing . . ." But then—and now my heart roars and crashes into reality like a tidal wave over land!—but then I'd probably never have needed to know about Kurtzes and . . . and Bialeks . . . and . . . and . . . Oh, what's the difference? Okay, so good people can be bad people sometimes, too. Surprise, surprise! And Erikson was right: it's tragic when ethical people do immoral stuff.

Hah! What a laugh!

You can't take *that* to the bank, mister!

I'm not sure I can hold out, disintegrating at the desk.

I should tell him everyone at school seems to know about their liaison, in case he doesn't realize that already.

Or ask why in God's name he didn't think we'd all get hung up in their blasted mess?

She knew about—dear God!—about the baby, too, even while they were . . . while they were . . . Lord Almighty! So that when it died . . . what in the heck would've stopped her . . . stopped her from feeling *she* was responsible, guilty . . . or . . . or . . . if not guilty, so embarrassed, she'd just have to quit?

He turns away from me.

"Please forgive me," he suddenly blurts out. "I shouldn't have let this go so far, forcing *you* to have to bring it to my—"

Damn, but I'd like to kick myself! Now I'm beginning to churn in the old direction wildly.

His blasted pain's completely mine again.

Before I know it, the words spurt from my mouth. "I'm so sorry, sir, about your . . ." I can't set *that* word loose. It clings like Super Glue to my tongue. "I am so-o-o sorry, sir."

He shrugs.

The teal blue eyes narrow, squinting at the fingers that have returned to interlacing themselves, only now so furiously, the knuckles crack like gunshots in the dark.

"Whoever thought"—he laughs a feeble, phony laugh—"whoever thought I'd be talking to a student this way?"

I know so exactly what he means, I turn to staring hot, searing holes into the spines of the books in his case, the blood boiling up into my face, past the knot stuck forever, it seems, in my throat.

When I don't answer, he goes on, a centimeter at a time, each of his words cloaked in an anguish that is either his or mine—I can't tell which any longer.

"Assure the others I'll talk to Dr. Bialek immediately—before we reassemble next week to begin our discussion of *Huckleberry Finn*."

My legs tremble.

I'm proud. I'm angry. I'm confused. All at one time.

He approaches me at the desk, picks up a paper clip that lies there, twists it open, snaps it in two in a kind of self-directed rage.

"Yessir," I say.

I've never been in a tighter situation. "Uh . . . we students, I know . . . well, we're not supposed to . . . you know . . . say things to teachers." The water's awfully deep, and I've never taken a course in lifesaving. On the other hand, it's the kind of emergency that can't stand long, convoluted debates. "But . . . er . . . but . . ." I cross my legs—knee holes be damned!—and pray for the best, this being the hardest thing I've ever had to say. "But I'm glad, Dr. Rogers. I'm glad you're going to tell her. Because this program's . . . uh . . . this program's . . ." Oh, God! That stupid Super Glue. "This program, sir, is . . . is your baby, too . . . and . . . and . . .

well . . . it's more alive than anything else in this school . . . and don't forget 'massive perseverance,' either!"

The blood's coursing through my veins so madly, I don't dare stay a second longer. Before he can do or say anything, I tear out of his office.

15

THE WEATHER'S turned warm, and the trees are budding. I'm soaking it all in—every beautiful inch of it—as I walk to Wardman's, despite being worried to death that Danny Stewart will blow his stack at me for arriving late again.

As I'm sticking my time card into the clock to punch in, sure enough, old Danny pops through the swinging doors.

"What'sit, Gallagher? Ya got yourself a boyfriend, keeping such late hours at school?"

My temperature shoots up.

On top of everything else, I've got to deal with him, too?

As I start to answer, he races off.

Whew!

But his reference to boyfriend puts me immediately in mind of Tuy, whom I call as soon as I can dig a quarter out of my pocket.

I explain my ambivalences following the talk with Dr. Rogers.

Tuy suggests we meet.

I offer up my house.

He's grateful.

He will come at eight, after dinner.

Now, at least, the family can meet him under "normal" circumstances before the cotillion.

I barely know what I'm doing for three hours. When they've passed, I rush home from work, screaming as I barge through the front door, "Tuy Nguyen's coming over so we can discuss the honors program. Let's eat!"

Frankly, I have no idea what I'm eating.

Frankly, I have no idea what Heather's mumbling to Matthew. Or, for that matter, what the meaning is of my father's pushing the splash of flowers away from the center of the table over to his side so that, for the first time in my memory, he and my mother have a clear view of each other.

Whatever it is we've had for dinner, I've bolted it down.

And then I race—I wish Spandexy Philbon could see me!—race, I say, upstairs to get dressed.

It's not a serene time, let me tell you!

I rummage through the closet and my bureau. My nerves jangle. My goose bumps cartwheel.

Suddenly, the old timidity rears its ugly head. I come across this jumper I got a year ago for my birthday, which I grew out of after exactly one wearing, and I want to die.

It's precisely the thing to wear tonight.

But, damn it! No matter how many different ways I try to stuff myself into the thing, my hips and rear end protrude like grotesques from a carnival.

I try on this skirt and blouse that look like my mother picked them up at a Salvation Army—so what if it doesn't fit?—sale.

Whichever way I wiggle, the skirt zipper won't lock, which means I could be sitting with Tuy quietly in the den, and bam!

But I refuse, absolutely refuse to meet him in jeans.

Beside myself with grief, I yell downstairs for Heather.

When she comes into my bedroom and sees the carnage on the floor, she strides right over to the closet, ransacks in it all the way to the rear, and then pulls it out—the hand-me-down party dress she gave me last spring when I begged her for it, but which I never bothered to get into for reasons you don't even have to think about.

"Try it," she says. "It's made just for you."

You cannot know the trepidation. The humiliation. The degradation.

She prods me. "This is what older sisters are for," she says.

Gingerly, as if I were holding a crystal vase, I raise the dress above my head and delicately rise up into it.

All the while, I've sucked my breath in and held it, so as not to cause the least bit of friction between me and the dress.

"*Voilà!*" Heather shouts. She smooths it down my sides, my hips, my back. "Fits like it was made to order."

I approach the mirror that hangs on the door, my eyes shut. Well, not altogether, but almost.

What little light gets through to the retina reveals this navy blue straight-line dress narrowing someone like you know who down to almost respectable size. It's not necessarily red chiffon slitted up the sides, but it'll do.

When Matthew yelps up from the base of the staircase that Tuy has arrived, I'm torn between cowering under my comforter and jumping out the bedroom window onto the patio roof below.

But always, always—no matter what's transpired since—Dr. Rogers's A to Z crisis line with its vees pops into view. I steel myself. Despite everything, he's left me no real choices. I can't avoid the crossroad. I've got to take one fork or another.

I trundle downstairs, praying they won't all be gathered below at the foot of the stairs like a bunch of voyeurs.

But, alas, except for Heather, who's following behind me, they are.

So of course I make the introductions.

Mom and Dad, I can see, are moderately shocked to discover that Tuy is not a WASP or, best of all possible worlds, Catholic.

Still, they fill me with pride at their cordiality during the introductions, at their civility in inquiring if Tuy would care for refreshments.

Shoot, Hope Gallagher! I tell myself. *Go for it!* "I've asked Tuy to the Sophomore Spring Cotillion, and he's said yes." I wait all of a second for whatever kind of volcanic eruption might take place. When the second passes, I say, "Don't you think that's great?"

They—Heather especially!—break into impenetrable, impervious smiles.

Like a chorus, they sing out, "Oh, that's marvelous."

Mom says, "You look wonderful in that dress."

Dad says, "Ditto that, sweetheart."

Matthew, fortunately, keeps quiet.

Hallelujah!

Tuy, who's wearing a very becoming turtleneck shirt and incredibly good-looking corduroy pants, bows!

"You are extremely gracious, Mr. and Mrs. Gallagher and Miss Heather and Mr. Matthew," he says.

It blows their minds. They bow in return and disappear into the kitchen.

Oh, boy, does this feel weird!

"Well," I manage, "here we are."

He's probably thinking, *Yes, so it is! But now what?*

"Yes, Hope," he says, "you are here now as well as I."

What I wouldn't do to have such—what?—equanimity of personality? Such serenity of mind.

It's of course occurred to me that we could hold our meeting in *my room*, but the ramifications of an action like that are unpredictable, countless.

So I lead Tuy to the den.

It's empty. There's plenty of view through the one long window above the couch, and there's a card table if we need to write.

We fidget for several seconds.

When I sit, Tuy follows, making, it seems to me, a concerted effort to place an appropriate amount of distance between the two of us. To be precise about it, I'm at one end of the couch; he's at the other.

He says, "So?"

It pleases me greatly that with his usual tactfulness he leaves it up to me to say as much or as little as *I* deem necessary. With him, of course, I haven't the least reluctance to spill my guts.

I pull my legs up on the couch—but not in any suggestive way—and run my hands through my hair, ending up, obviously, at the split ends, which against my better judgment, I linger at.

Finally, I repeat virtually the entire conversation with Dr. Rogers.

Tuy suddenly turns very serious, the change in his face making him look even nicer than I remembered, and I get this . . . uh . . . well orangy or pinkish feeling all over.

Then, shutting his eyes and pressing his lips together, he meditates a moment before bowling me over totally by paraphrasing Erikson: "The source of all tragedy, Erikson says, is when an otherwise ethical man commits an immoral act."

Have two human beings ever been more in sync than Tuy Nguyen and Hope Gallagher, I ask you? Have they?

"Lord, Tuy," I scream, scooting a fraction of an inch closer. "That's exactly what came to my mind when Dr. Rogers told me everything!"

Tuy breaks into this contagious, infectious grin that rips me apart.

"As in our program itself, there is a oneness to everything in the universe that if we constantly seek out we shall find."

Good God! What a mind! What sensitivity!

I pull my dress down even more fully over my legs, trying awfully hard to keep my calves from looking as huge as it seems to me they look by squeezing the two of them up as tight as I can against each other. But no matter how hard I push, they refuse to respond.

The difference, though, is that Tuy's so engrossed in the important things in life, he doesn't seem to be the least bit concerned about the thickness of my legs at all, which makes me suddenly realize that flaws alone don't make a person, any more than talents alone do.

"I think we've all been too hypercritical of Dr. Bialek, too," I say.

Tuy's eyes light up.

"You are absolutely right," he says.

"Do you think it'd be presumptuous of me to go see her to let her know that some of us haven't exactly gone out of our way to give her a chance, either?"

"That is a fantastic suggestion. Yes, yes, Hope. I continue to think you make a fine spokesperson for the group."

I can't wait for that cotillion, so help me God!

16

SHE SEEMS a lot smaller to me than she does in front of a class, the following week as I come upon her sitting all alone at her desk. Smaller and, somehow, a lot less fearsome.

And, as much as I hate to admit it, she's also a lot prettier up close than from the distance of the back row or the conference table.

For one thing, every bit of her is in just the right proportion. Her nose, for instance, fits exactly the way it ought to on a face that's only slightly longer than it is wide. And there's just exactly the right amount of space between the nose and lips and the lips and chin, as though all three features had been chiseled out of marble by a sculptor.

She's not too showy, either, in her dress, confident enough, I suppose, not to have to wear special effects like, say, tons of gold necklaces or earrings down to her shoulders.

Nuts!

Still, watching her from outside her office door while she's bending over some papers on her desk, if I'm going to be honest about it, I have to say I . . . Well, *hate* wasn't ever the right word . . . but it's the only one I can think of.

I knock on the door, and she looks up from her work, catching sight—wouldn't you know it?—of my jeans even before my face.

"Oh," she says. "It's you."

The greeting doesn't augur well.

I'll bet anything *he* hasn't spoken to her yet.

Lord Almighty!

What do I do then?

"May I speak to you?" I say, avoiding her name, not maliciously or anything but torn because I'm not sure it wouldn't be dishonest of me to pronounce it.

"What can I do for you?" she as cautiously avoiding "Ms. Gallagher" responds.

What's shocking is the absence from her voice of that bitchiness we've all grown accustomed to.

Maybe he *has* spoken to her already?

"Uh . . . well . . ." I'm really forcing each word out now.

The trouble is, What am I here for?

To apologize . . . for nothing?

For harboring green-eyed, monstrous thoughts?

To complain about the past, if, in fact, the past is over?

To say . . . to say . . . dear God, if someone had done something like that to me, I'd have freaked out, too, in front of students or not?

To wonder how a person allows herself to be . . . Oh, well, what's the difference? And besides, what gives me the right?

It's just not all that simple. All black. All white. So can we try from now on?

"Why don't you take a seat?" she says.

Which I do.

"I just wanted to say—" I say, then stop, at a loss.

"Not to tell anyone to shut up anymore, or that they're irrelevant?" she says softly, almost as if she were chanting, muttering a litany.

I don't know which way to turn first, this new twist throwing me for a loop, this almost too unreal, too sudden to believe transformation.

Out of nowhere, I hear myself saying, "Dr. Rogers practically single-handedly saved me."

"I know," she says to my utter, my complete astonishment.

"How?" I retort. I don't know if I'm supposed to feel honored or betrayed or what, realizing that he's shared our secret.

"When he started the program and asked each of

us to name the students we thought ought to be in it, he made a very—how shall I put it?—a very extravagant point of informing all of us about you as a standard we might use in making our own recommendations."

Oh. I knew it! I knew it all the time. Erikson. Gandhi. Love. Mutuality. My arms, crossed over my chest, squeeze the smithereens out of me. *How can I possibly harbor doubts about you, Dr. Rogers? How in God's name could I doubt you for a minute?*

"But how . . ." I want to ask about the baby, how she could—knowing what it meant to him and the program—how could she do what she did, no matter how she felt, especially when he chose her and she obviously accepted?

A look comes over her face that, to put it mildly, is as bereft, as forlorn, as anguished as his was last week.

I'd have bet every one of my father's Michigan Avenue clients this woman did not have such looks anywhere in her repertoire, which just goes to show you how little we can know about people we think we know.

Still and all, I feel so sick, I want to barge out of there, just to get away from all of it.

But she grabs my hand from across the desk.

Her palms are sweating a mile a minute.

"Please let me try to explain."

I bend to the tiny bit of pressure of her hand.

"Um . . ." She's staring at everything in the office but me. "You see . . ." The catch in her voice rises up from some deep, long-forsaken niche in her soul where, once, love or caring got trampled on and so now they come to the surface only reluctantly. "Dr. Rogers . . . Everett . . . has spoken to me about the class's reactions to my acting out." She stops to study my fingers, which she has still not let go of. "I'm sure I don't have to tell you all the details. . . . So many people seem to know so much already. . . . But whatever happened, I had no right, in public, to behave as I did. It was as unspeakable and inexcusable as . . . Well, it just was, and that's all there is to it. I lost my . . . It won't happen again. . . ."

I'm having some difficulty believing what I'm hearing.

"A part of me knows it's not a question of fault or blame. It's human nature." She chuckles timidly. "For a while, I thought I . . . we . . . were above all that. But not a one of us is. As for me, because of his child's death, instead of being kinder and gentler, I became bestial, infuriated like a treed animal under siege. Unfortunately, that's *my* nature."

I'm trying to put myself in her position, and it occurs to me if Tuy . . . if Tuy would not show up on cotillion night and then I found him at the Women's Club with Doty or Tammy or someone . . . God, I don't know what I'd do!

"No, it's not," I say. I'd like to think I've suddenly, magically turned into an incarnation of the new Golden Rule. But I'm shaking too much. And if I'm going to be honest, I can't really say I've suddenly turned to loving her.

She squeezes my hand.

I get up and am about to thank her for giving me time.

But she beats me to the punch.

"Dr. Rogers . . . Everett . . . he was absolutely right about you, you know."

I wish I knew what I was absolutely right about!

17

DR. ROGERS strides to his desk, deposits his books, and takes up his position on the corner of it.

"To *The Adventures of Huckleberry Finn*," he says.

He looks older to me.

Tuy and I have told Joshua and Doty and Tammy and Tommy only what we've had to.

As he begins to speak, I think I hear the Stradivarius back in his voice and furtively eye the others, looking to them for some sign of confirmation.

They're clearly uncertain.

"What," Dr. Rogers says, "what's the connection between the dying Kurtz's muttering 'The Horror!

The Horror!' in *Heart of Darkness* and Huck's deciding to tear up the letter he's written to his aunt telling her where the runaway slave Jim is?''

Darn, if the twitch doesn't begin!

Darn, if my heart's not already racing, anticipating, yearning for the questions to begin!

Here we go again!

Unlike that very first session when he asked about Erikson and it seemed to take forever before Tuy spoke up, this time hands fly up all over the place, including that of yours truly.

Once again, despite everything, I'm transported directly into Dr. Rogers's shoes, realizing—as Rosa once put it—how much Huck and Kurtz and Erikson—and now Drs. Rogers and Bialek, me and Tuy and the others—have in common and how "one" all knowledge is.

I swear to God!

Exhilarated?

You bet!

Rhapsodic?

Indubitably!

But stuff's happened, too.

White's become a little more black, black a little more white.

My attention's straying.

I'm losing some of Dr. Rogers's words thinking ahead to how things'll be cotillion night.

But that's okay.

Because when he points to me, the palpitations

abate somewhat. And the goose bumps, too. But not appreciably.

"Ms. Gallagher?" he says. His lips open slightly. They form a circle!

Oh, Lord!

"Hope?" he says.

I'm breathing hard again.

I'm going to die!

"Ahem," I start. "Yessir," I mutter. "Um . . . uh . . . Huck . . . er . . ." Oh, Joshua. How you must have to suffer!

Hope! My God! Dr. Rogers called me Hope!

Heather, how I wish you were here!

"The . . . uh . . . connection is that Huck's in a situation . . . um . . . that calls for a serious moral and ethical decision."

I can hear the words coming out of my mouth, but they surely don't sound like my words. The voice surely doesn't sound like my voice.

Despite everything and against my better judgment, my soul's been inhabited by Everett Rogers again!

A torrent follows.

"Huck's been taught to believe that slavery's right and good and he believes what he's been taught, yes? Just as Kurtz believed that it was right for a white man to go into Africa to *civilize*"—I stress *civilize* exactly as I know he, Dr. Rogers would—"to civilize what *he* called the 'brutes,' the black men. Only . . . only, in each case, Huck's and

Kurtz's, they end up following their hearts, not their heads. Huck may have been taught that slavery is right, but his heart tells him it's wrong, that the black man Jim is a fine human being, finer than many whites Huck has met, which is why Huck decides he'd rather go to hell himself than to turn Jim in to the authorities."

I make a move to hide my thighs, then decide to heck with it.

"Kurtz, on the other hand," I go on, "Kurtz's goodness is entirely in his head. The moment his environment and circumstances provide the opportunity, he becomes more barbaric than the people he has the arrogance to think it's his mission to civilize."

There's this thunderous ovation.

My blood pressure must be rising out of sight, I'm so embarrassed.

If I make it to the cotillion, it'll be a miracle.

I look Dr. Rogers straight in the eye. The teal blue shows signs of gleaming again.

"So . . . so . . . Dr. Rogers, sir . . . what you—I'm sorry—what *they* all have in common is that in the end, no matter what anybody says to them or does to them, even life itself, they . . . er . . . learn to listen to their hearts. And . . . and . . . sometimes our hearts lead us the right way, sometimes not. But . . . but the thing is . . . it's okay. We're human, that's all."

There's more clapping, but frankly it's just noise now in the background.

"Sometimes . . . uh . . . someone or something tries to drive a wedge or something between what our hearts want to do and what our heads keep telling us we have to do. That's . . . I don't know for sure . . . but I think that's when the troubles begin."

Dr. Rogers approaches my seat.

He says, speaking to the class, "It's not so much that language is man's last hope as that *Hope, here, ought to be mankind's only language.* Your answer's right on the money."

My paper being his and my secret, the others may not understand, but so what?

After class, Tuy says to me, "It was very wise that you invited me to your house before the cotillion, Hope. I must tell you I was quite nervous about meeting your family. Now that I have met them, it will not be so difficult to come again."

Oh, Tuy! How right you are!

I'm wondering if, when we go to Dr. Bialek's class later in the day, she'll have something to say to the group like what she said to me.

Tuy, reading my mind, says, "Even if Dr. Bialek doesn't apologize to the group, it will no longer be the end of the world, do you not think so, Hope?"

Once more, my impulsiveness gets the better of me.

Teeming students in the corridors or not, I get up on my tiptoes and kiss him on the cheek.

I don't care what anybody says. Sometimes, it's plain good to be a little impulsive. It's not the end of the world, for God's sake!